P[...]

JUST L[...]

The enigma of the [...]
Sheena Frankly-Aw[...]
has long fascinated Annabel. But even she wouldn't
have guessed that it would be the pranks of a bored
donkey that would set her and her best friend Kate
on the trail which leads to the resolution of so baffling
a conundrum. And along the way they find themselves in some extraordinary and hilarious situations.

Then, in the second of these two stories, Annabel
adopts a 'new attitude' to life with the most astound-
ing and bewildering results.

Annabel is back with all her innocent idealism and
astute awareness of the ways of the adults of Addendon. And the result is another volume of riotous fun
and wickedly observant humour.

Alan Davidson's irrepressible heroine first appeared
in *A Friend Like Annabel*, also published in Puffin.
Married with four children and living in Dorset, Alan
Davidson is also the author of the marvellously gripping story *The Bewitching of Alison Allbright*.

Another book by Alan Davidson

A FRIEND LIKE ANNABEL

ALAN DAVIDSON

* * * * *

Just like
Annabel

PUFFIN BOOKS

PUFFIN BOOKS

Published by the Penguin Group
27 Wrights Lane, London W8 5TZ, England
Viking Penguin Inc., 40 West 23rd Street, New York, New York 10010, USA
Penguin Books Australia Ltd, Ringwood, Victoria, Australia
Penguin Books Canada Ltd, 2801 John Street, Markham, Ontario, Canada L3R 1B4
Penguin Books (NZ) Ltd, 182–190 Wairau Road, Auckland 10, New Zealand

Penguin Books Ltd, Registered Offices: Harmondsworth, Middlesex, England

First published by Granada Publishing 1983
Published by Viking Kestrel 1988
Published in Puffin Books 1989
1 3 5 7 9 10 8 6 4 2

Reproduced, printed and bound in Great Britain by
Hazell Watson & Viney Limited
Member of BPCC plc
Aylesbury, Bucks, England
Filmset in Trump Mediaeval

Contents

*****

For Anna

Annabel
and the enigma of
Sheena Franks-Walters

*****

Chapter 1

*****

'Whoever,' Annabel was to say later with much eye-rolling and wise shaking of the head, 'whoever would have guessed that the enigma of Sheena Franks-Walters would finally be resolved because Mr Loader's donkey, Eastbourne, knocked Mrs da Susa over when she was on her way to Willers one morning? Would you, Kate? Would you have guessed? Honestly now?'

No, Kate was to admit. She would never have guessed.

'It's like the opening to one of those articles you read, isn't it, Kate. *What is the amazing connection between Eastbourne the donkey and the Franks-Walters family?*'

Annabel had long been intrigued by the enigma of Sheena Franks-Walters – or Sheena Frankly-Awful as she was sometimes called. Put briefly, it was thus:

Why did Sheena Franks-Walters, their fellow pupil in the Third Year at Lord Willoughby's School, Addendon, whose parents were the owners of Addendon Court and so wealthy that they could obviously afford to send her to the best school in the country, come instead to a dump like Willers to mix with and be dragged down by people such as Damian Price, Richard White, Miles Noggins and Justine Bird, to name but a few of the innumerable undesirables?

Why, every morning at five to nine, did she step from a vintage limousine drawn up outside the school gates, give a gracious nod and a dimpled smile to the chauffeur, Bennion, who handed her a leather case containing her books, smoked salmon sandwiches, flask of freshly-ground coffee etc. and then, apparently oblivious of any cat-calls or jeers, pad her way into school, there to begin another day of sweetly-smiling, uncommunicative inactivity in the corner desk?

There had to be a reason and Annabel wanted to know it. However, the aura of bland unapproachableness that surrounded Sheena made direct investigation difficult if not impossible and it wasn't until the affair of Mr Loader's donkey that Annabel summoned up the determination to do something about it.

But to begin at the beginning . . .

Annabel Bunce and her best friend Kate Stocks had had a sort of nodding acquaintance with Eastbourne for some time but it was in, of all surprising places, the *Smart Set* hairdressing salon on Gamble Street that they first entered into a closer relationship with him.

It was their practice to go to the *Smart Set* together, approximately once every six weeks, so that they would have each other to chat to while having their hair trimmed.

Their hair was not, of course, attended to by Fabian, the renowned proprietor of the *Smart Set*. He was busy with the important customers in the main salon. Annabel and Kate, being of no importance whatsoever and whose custom he would no doubt have been delighted to lose, were consigned to a small back room which also housed a stove, cups and saucers, brooms and other necessary but unglamorous impedimenta. From there they were able to hear the refined murmurings and tinkle of coffee-cups coming from the main salon while having their hair trimmed by Natalie, the most incompetent of the trainees, whom Fabian was unable to get rid of because of the Employment Act.

Sometimes, between their trims, or even during their trims, Natalie would break off to make coffee, put it on a tray and disappear with it into the main salon without, naturally, offering them any. It was on such an occasion, just when Natalie had disappeared while about to start Annabel's trim, that Annabel realized that a donkey was looking at her through a window.

'A-a-ah!' she drooled 'Look, Kate. Just look.'

The window was a small one, almost unnoticeable, with curtains half drawn across it. The donkey's head, motionless as a portrait as it gazed steadily into the room, was placed centrally between the curtains.

'He wants to come in,' said Annabel, getting up from the chair in her gown.

She drew the curtains aside and peered out at him.

'It's Eastbourne,' said Kate. 'That must be Mr Loader's yard out there.'

They both knew Mr Loader slightly, mainly through saying hallo to him when passing the open window of his home, an ancient building, formerly the Smithy, on the corner of Gamble Street and Stumbury. Mr Loader, though now retired, had been a blacksmith in the days when Addendon had been a large village rather than a small town.

Annabel approved of him, partly because he was a friend of Mr Rumator, the groundsman at Lord Willoughby's – and any friend of Mr Rumator's was bound to be all right – and partly for the very reasons that he was disapproved of by some members of the Addendon Town Council.

Both Mr Loader and his home were considered by these members to be eyesores, an affront to

Addendon and the vision of a well-ordered, modern small town which they saw rising from the outdated Addendon of the past. Mr Loader, and his home, were a mess.

This applied particularly to the small garden, or yard, which lay next to his cottage and fronted on to Gamble Street, from which it was separated by a broken, patched-up fence. Mr Loader was an obsessive collector and hoarder and his yard was piled high with what some would see as interesting bric-à-brac and others as old rubbish. When any house had been pulled down in Addendon, Mr Loader had been there to pick over the ruins and rescue old tiles, beams, sinks, anything which he might subsequently be able to sell for a song.

Mixed up with this were old bicycles, farm equipment and other items which had at some time taken his fancy and which were perhaps repairable.

Around and over this huge heap, his hens clucked and scratched and laid their eggs, bossed around by a strutting and aggressive cockerel. When they were bored with this, they would slip through the gaps in the fence and forage out into Gamble Street, the cockerel having an occasional peck at a passer-by.

The other residents of Mr Loader's yard were a cat, some rabbits in a hutch and Eastbourne. Eastbourne was very reflective by nature and would stand for long periods just thinking. Annabel and Kate had sometimes fallen to guessing what it was he was thinking about and had leaned over the fence to ask him and throw him some titbit.

Mostly Eastbourne would do his thinking within the confines of the yard but very occasionally he would do it with his head hanging over the fence. This could be alarming to the patrons of the *Smart Set* which had the misfortune to occupy premises next door to the Smithy; one wall, that with the small window in it, being the boundary wall to Mr Loader's yard.

Whether it was the particular hair lacquer that the *Smart Set* used is difficult to say but certainly Eastbourne, while ignoring patrons on their way there, would sometimes take a great interest in them when they emerged, if they were coming in his direction, craning his neck and apparently trying to take in the aroma. Whether he merely wanted to sniff the hair, lick it or bite it was impossible to say because, sensibly, none of the *Smart Set*'s customers wanted to put it to the test, preferring to sidle past along the edge of the pavement. But it certainly destroyed the feeling of glamour and well-being so carefully and expensively fostered within the *Smart Set*'s sumptuous salon. It and Mr Loader made uneasy neighbours.

All this was highly offensive to Mr Loader's critics on the Town Council and of course to Fabian himself. They would dearly have liked to get rid of Mr Loader, his donkey, his hens and his rubbish and consign him to some bungalow on the outer reaches of one of Addendon's furthest-flung estates. Mr Loader, however, had lived in the Smithy all his life and firmly intended spending his remaining years there in the company of his beloved Eastbourne, his chief confidant since his wife had died some three years ago.

This, then, was the donkey which now confronted Annabel and Kate through Fabian's window.

'He wants to have his hair done,' cooed Annabel, soppily. 'Doesn't oo then. Is it all tangled and itchy and needs a set?'

Saying which she pushed aside the little curtain and, in order to speak to Eastbourne more intimately and give him a pat, unlatched the window and opened it.

Instantly, Eastbourne pushed his head in through the window.

'Eastbourne!' said Kate, in alarm. 'Bad donkey! Out!'

Eastbourne paid no attention. Annabel placed a hand on either side of his head and tried to ease it back but he was immoveable. Having gained entry so unexpectedly to this rich source of interest he was not going to retreat without a struggle. Possibly it was the strong scent of the lacquer within that was attracting him. To have come across the origins of it was, perhaps, like Stanley realizing that he had found the source of the Congo.

Kate came to Annabel's assistance but nothing made any impression on Eastbourne who continued to strain forward. As they struggled silently, the clink of cups and saucers and well-bred murmurs of 'Thank you so much' could be heard faintly in the salon. Natalie was distributing the coffee. Fabian was continuing to fiddle with hair while Rome burned. This might have continued indefinitely except that Eastbourne suddenly realized that his head was stuck in the window frame. This alarmed him. Baring his teeth, he proceeded to blare out a shattering and ear-splitting bellow. Caught by it at close quarters, Annabel and Kate fell backwards. From the salon came screams and cries of confusion and alarm and the sound of crashing coffee-cups.

Eastbourne waited only until Fabian dashed into the room to see what was going on before violently withdrawing his head. Its disappearance was quite impressive. It popped out like a cork and was gone.

As Annabel and Kate were to realize later, this incident was to have most unfortunate consequences. It was what finally made Fabian determined to get rid of Mr Loader and his whole menagerie. This had been

14

in his mind for some time but now his attitude hardened. He took the precaution of screwing down the little window and keeping the curtains drawn, then bided his time, waiting for an opportunity.

It was noticeable that, after the curtains had been drawn, Eastbourne took to doing more of his thinking with his head hanging over the fence, presumably having to make the most of the one diversion that remained to him. He also appeared, as Annabel observed one day when pausing to pat him, to be thinking still more deeply as if, she said, the experience had embittered him.

Annabel felt very guilty about opening the window. As she and Kate were aware, it had led to an increase in tension in Gamble Street and also to Eastbourne being denied a simple pleasure, the lack of which might make him even naughtier in future.

Fabian was making a similar calculation.

Eastbourne continued to take a great interest in the *Smart Set*'s departing customers but still without giving Fabian quite the necessary ammunition to fire the devastating broadside that he dreamed of. That, he believed, must await the intervention of some lucky chance, probably in the shape of some idiot of a passer-by who would be silly enough to get into some sort of contretemps with Eastbourne.

Enter Mrs Muriel da Susa MA (Oxon), BSc (Soc.) (London), Adv. Dip. Ed. (London), Deputy Head of Lord Willoughby's School.

Chapter 2

*****

Mrs da Susa's route to school in the morning (she lived in Woodland Drive in a modern bungalow called 'Napoli', after the city where she had met her husband) took her along Stumbury, turning left into Gamble Street; that is, directly past the Smithy. She had been using this route for some years without incident but one morning as she was passing Mr Loader's yard deep in thought – 'no doubt', Annabel was to say, 'thinking about whom she could harrass and irritate that morning' – Eastbourne, who had been doing his thinking with his head hanging over the fence, suddenly brought his nose up sharply and nudged her on the shoulder. The suddenness of it caused her to stagger and fall over, dropping the books she was carrying.

Mrs da Susa was naturally very annoyed by this and after hoisting herself to her feet with, no doubt, as Annabel was to comment, a good deal of clucking and snorting, she banged at the door of the Smithy intending to give Mr Loader a piece of her mind.

When after some minutes she received no reply, she realized that the front door, which gave directly on to the pavement, was nailed up. She would have to go to the back door, approached via the yard. She made to do this then realized that Eastbourne was now standing with his head hanging over the gate, apparently hoping to knock her over again. She therefore went off fuming.

That evening she told her husband sharply to be a man and go and complain for her. He, in some perhaps justifiable confusion, brought up her views on women's lib at which point she asked him what sort of a man it was that refused to protect his wife and ordered him to be off. Perhaps she hoped that, even if he were ineffective, Eastbourne would knock him over too and save her the trouble. Mr da Susa accordingly squared his shoulders and departed.

He did not return for some three hours by which time Mrs da Susa had become quite anxious about him. Perhaps former blacksmiths were not good persons to tangle with. Then Mr da Susa reappeared smiling happily and carrying an old bicycle without any wheels. No, Eastbourne had not knocked him over – it was clear from his changing expression that Mr da Susa had forgotten the original point of his mission – Eastbourne had in fact greeted him very amiably and as for Mr Loader, he was a most pleasant and interesting person who had let him have this old bicycle for five pence – or, to be accurate, for a shilling since Mr Loader did not recognize decimal money. It needed only some wheels.

Mrs da Susa fumed and decided to let the incident pass. Several days went by during which she kept a wary look-out for Eastbourne on her way to school. Eastbourne had, however, apparently decided to return to doing his thinking within the yard. On the fifth day, Mrs da Susa relaxed and forgot to be on guard.

Eastbourne promptly knocked her over again.

Incensed, Mrs da Susa contemplated contacting Authority in order to have the nuisance stopped. However, she didn't really want to make trouble for Mr Loader – and a few moments' reflection told her that the forces ranged against him, in the shape of Fabian and the harder members of the Town Council, would be relentless, given grounds upon which to strike. She decided that she needed someone in some sort of authority, but not too much – enough to subdue Mr Loader but not enough to pose a serious threat to him, someone with discretion and tact.

Accordingly, that same evening, she called at the Mill Lane home of Mrs Winnie Stringer who, though a self-important busybody, did perhaps have those qualities to a degree, being a member of the Town Council and not without a certain kindness of heart.

These two formidable pillars of the Addendon establishment consulted in Mrs Stringer's sitting-room.

'I know', said Mrs da Susa, 'that you are a person who can be relied upon to handle this issue with sensitivity. A friendly word, perhaps, in your position of authority as a councillor, but quite unofficial . . . I would not want the poor old fellow to get into trouble or be parted from his donkey.'

'You have', Mrs Stringer assured her, 'come to the right person. Without, I hope, being boastful, I do flatter myself that where others might move perhaps in a heavy-handed fashion, I am able to handle a situation with delicacy. I'll tell you what I'll do. I know that Mrs Janes, of Meals-on-Wheels, takes Mr Loader his dinner on Saturdays. This week I shall take it instead and we shall have a cosy little chat as he eats it. I think that would be perfect.'

As it happened, on that Saturday Annabel and Kate were again in the *Smart Set* for a trim, six weeks having passed since their last visit. They were, there-fore, close at hand to witness the climax of this drama, though they did not actually see the arrival of Mrs Stringer, Annabel being seated in the chair at the

18

time, undergoing Natalie's inexpert ministrations while Kate patiently awaited her turn.

Unfortunately, Mrs Stringer made a mistake. This was because Mrs Janes had neglected to brief her properly.

What Mrs Stringer didn't know was that it was Mrs Janes' practice to deliver the meal not at Mr Loader's back door but via his window on the Stumbury side of the house. She didn't know why Mr Loader had this preference but he did and she was happy to oblige.

In fact, Mr Loader had this preference because he didn't want the meal himself. Though conscious of and grateful for the kindly thought behind it, he was perfectly capable of cooking for himself and didn't, in any case, like Cauliflower Cheese, the Saturday meal.

So having received it through the window, he would take it to the back door and give it to Eastbourne, who adored it. He would then return to his own favourite Saturday meal of well-hung roast pheasant with bread sauce and sauté potatoes.

(The pheasant, like his favourite Friday dish of grilled trout and his Thursday favourite, *Pigeon en cocotte Normande*, was poached from the Franks-Walters estates. It was because of his shyness about explaining this that Mrs Janes had first got the impression that he was going hungry.)

He knew – as Mrs Stringer did not – that to deliver the meal to the back door would invite the premature attention of Eastbourne and make him over-excited.

Mrs Stringer parked her car on Gamble Street – well away from the corner where the double yellow lines are for she took care at all times not to transgress the law – and, carrying the meal while firmly holding its cover in place, bustled importantly towards the Smithy for her cosy chat. While passing the *Smart Set* she was noticed by Fabian, who happened to be glancing out of the window at the time. He wondered what the old fool was up to now.

Eastbourne was in deep thought with his head hanging over the fence when he saw Mrs Stringer approach or, rather, he became aware of the approach of the Cauliflower Cheese with Mrs Stringer in attendance.

Thrilled that it was being brought to him direct, without having to undergo the usual formalities, he expressed his excitement by throwing back his head, baring his teeth and emitting a huge bellow. This was heard by Fabian who, putting two and two together, and sensing that his patience might be about to be rewarded, left the customer he was attending to and dashed to the door to see what was happening.

It was also heard by Annabel and Kate. Annabel was the quicker off the mark. Ignoring the risk of being stabbed by Natalie's scissors, she leapt up, scrambled to the little window and pulled aside the curtains so as to be able to peer through into Mr Loader's yard and see what Eastbourne was doing.

Eastbourne was excitedly gambolling along the inside of the fence, keeping level with the startled Mrs Stringer and making grabs at the Cauliflower Cheese which she was attempting to hold away from him without having to step off the pavement into the path of passing cars. They got as far as the gate in this way.

Here, with that dogged persistence for which she was noted, Mrs Stringer refused to be daunted and attempted to enter the yard. At this point, Eastbourne managed to get his nose to the dish, first pushing off the cover then, as the agitated Mrs Stringer tried to retrieve that, knocking the plate out of her hand. As she stood looking helplessly down at the Cauliflower Cheese, now splodged on the pavement, Eastbourne –

beside himself with excitement – nudged her with his nose and knocked her over.

All this was witnessed by Fabian, who was now hurrying towards the scene, and by Annabel and Kate who were emerging from the *Smart Set* in his wake, Annabel still in her gown.

(It could hardly be coincidence, Annabel was to maintain later, that of all the people in Addendon, it was Mrs da Susa and Mrs Stringer whom he had chosen to knock over. Surely this gave the final answer to those people who maintain that animals have no intelligence. Clearly, it had been in Eastbourne's mind all along to conduct a campaign to clean up Addendon of some of its worst elements. This was what he had been thinking about and planning for so long in the yard.)

Stifling any cries of triumph or glee, Fabian ran, with much hypocritical tut-tutting and many exclamations of sympathy, to help Mrs Stringer to her feet, a task which soon silenced him and brought the sweat out on his brow. While he was doing this, Mr Loader's cockerel, stimulated by all the excitement, stalked out through a gap in the fence and pecked him on the leg. Straightening up quickly, he felt hot breath on the back of his neck, followed by a raking tongue. Eastbourne, deprived of his Cauliflower Cheese, was at least having the consolation of getting close enough to the *Smart Set*'s lacquer to give it the examination it deserved. No longer caring what happened to Mrs Stringer, Fabian allowed her to slump on to the pavement again and then, floundering, trod on the Cauliflower Cheese, skidded and joined her.

At this point Mr Loader emerged from his back door, a wondering expression on his face, to see what was going on. He was deeply disturbed by what he saw.

He knew that Eastbourne had gone too far, that he had played into the hands of those forces which were ranged against him. Now they would 'get' him. And if they 'got' Eastbourne they would 'get' Mr Loader, too. He wouldn't stay in the Smithy if Eastbourne had to go. They had been together too long.

Annabel and Kate realized this, too.

'Oh, Eastbourne,' said Annabel, 'you are a *very* naughty donkey.'

On the following Monday Mr Poynton-Green, Clerk to the Addendon Council, arrived at the Smithy, prodded by an excited Fabian. He was carrying an umbrella – although it was a dry day – with which to fend off any possible advances from Eastbourne. It was his unpleasant duty, he informed Mr Loader, to tell him that he had one month in which to find a new home for Eastbourne, failing which, appropriate and most undesirable action would have to be taken under the bye-laws in order to achieve the same result.

Annabel heard the news the same afternoon from Mr Rumator and promptly burst into tears.

'It's partly my fault,' she wailed to Kate. 'That's what makes it even worse. I shouldn't have opened that window. We've got to do something, Kate. What can we do?'

'I don't know,' said Kate.

They were walking out of the school at the time. Not far away, Sheena Franks-Walters was stepping into her vintage limousine. Although she didn't know it, Sheena's part in this drama was about to begin.

Mrs da Susa's was completed. As she exits, left, having completed her ignominious role to no one's satisfaction other than Fabian's, Sheena Franks-Walters waits in the wings, right, about to burst on stage.

Chapter 3

*****

Instead of going straight home, Annabel and Kate called on Mr Loader. Annabel said the least they could do was to try to offer him some comfort and show him the whole world wasn't against him.

Eastbourne was standing in the yard. His head seemed to be hanging lower than in earlier days. Annabel patted his nose and gave him a carrot she had brought him.

'Your clean-up campaign was a good try,' she told him, sympathetically, 'but the job was too big for one donkey. You didn't stand a chance.'

They had never been in the yard before and it was interesting. They were now able to see that behind the pile of bric-à-brac lay the cavernous opening to a large, dark shed in the interior of which was an anvil, surrounded by further bric-à-brac. It was the old blacksmith's shop. Not so many years ago, there would have been the glow of fire in there and a muscular, shirt-sleeved Mr Loader wielding his mighty hammer.

Annabel heaved a little sigh and looked pensive. Five minutes later they were in Mr Loader's sitting-room, drinking tea with him.

'We called him Eastbourne,' said Mr Loader, 'because the missus and I had just come back from holiday there when we first got him. He was a seaside donkey himself. Used to give rides on the

23

beach in summer. We looked after him for the owner one winter and got so fond of him we bought him.

'Of course,' he added, after a sip of his tea, 'we had the grazing then.' He offered Annabel and Kate some home-made madeira cake.

It was a very old sitting-room with a beamed ceiling, inglenook fireplace and bulging white walls. It was a pity that the traffic roared by right outside the window. Kate was surprised by how many books there were around the room: beautifully bound sets of Dickens and Jane Austen and the Brontës, books on metallurgy, cookery, natural and local history, books on many things. Mr Loader was clearly a man of wide interests.

'He has been naughty, though, hasn't he?' said Kate. 'Couldn't you have built a higher fence?'

'Didn't have the heart,' said Mr Loader. 'Poor old Eastbourne. It's already boring enough having to stand in that little yard all day. I couldn't shut him in altogether. But perhaps I should have done.'

He lumbered to his feet.

'Boredom, that's the whole trouble,' he said. 'Everything was fine till a couple of years ago. That's when we lost the grazing. I'll show you.'

Annabel and Kate rose and followed him through a lobby into another room, a small scullery with an old brown flat-bottomed sink in it and a lot of bottles of home-made wine and beer on shelves.

'Look through there,' he said, indicating the small window.

They peered at a large, irregular open space which lay next to Mr Loader's house and yard on the Stumbury side. It was separated from the yard by some newish-looking lapboard fencing, which Kate had noticed beside the blacksmith's shed, and from

Stumbury by a stone wall. It was a riot of matted grass and weeds.

'That was the grazing,' said Mr Loader. 'Eastbourne was very happy there – been miserable since he left it. That's what makes him snappy. The hens were very happy there as well. We were all happy. I used to grow a lot of things there.'

He gazed out, nostalgic for a golden past.

'Who owns it?' asked Kate.

'Little Miss Wilkin *used* to own it. She lived over there.' He nodded towards a thatched cottage on the other side of the open space. 'She let us have the grazing and I did her house repairs and kept her in eggs and vegetables and the occasional trou – the occasional nice piece of fish or game. Though never out of season,' he added, vaguely but virtuously. 'Very nice arrangement, it was.'

'And now?' said Kate.

'She died, that was very sad that was, and left it to some cousin. Next I knew it had been sold. For a fortune, I heard. Miss Wilkin would have turned in her grave. Couldn't believe my ears. Then that new fence suddenly appeared and I was told I couldn't use it any more.'

'Who said that?'

'Chap from Hazelford's, the Estate Agents in the High Street. They're managing it for the new owners. If you can call it managing!' he added, gloomily. 'They don't even cut the weeds. He said the new owners are somebody called "The Hackney and Wester Ross Property Company".'

'"Hackney and Wester Ross?"' repeated Kate, puzzled. 'What have they got to do with Addendon?'

'What's Hackney got to do with Wester Ross, come to that,' said Annabel. 'One's in London and the other's in the north of Scotland.'

'Dunno,' said Mr Loader, still more gloomily. 'The

way these property companies carry on is beyond me. I don't even know what they want the land for. Look at it. Doing nothing with it.'

He turned away. 'Still, that's nothing to do with me any more. No use looking back. I've got to deal with the problem I've got now. Come and have another piece of cake.'

'Isn't there anybody who can help?' Annabel asked when they were back in his sitting-room.

'I did think about asking Mr Franks-Walters,' said Mr Loader, a little shyly, 'but it wouldn't be any use.'

'Mr Franks-Walters?' Annabel repeated, interested by this reference to Sheena's father. 'Why him?'

'Well, he's the sort of squire of Addendon, isn't he. A gentleman. He might have the measure of the people who are after me and Eastbourne. He used to be a Member of Parliament and yet he's a man of the people, too. His daughter goes to the local school, doesn't she?'

'She's in our class,' said Kate.

'Is she now? Yes, you see, a man of the people. The Franks-Walters are part of England's history. They've lived at Addendon for seven hundred years. And they've always looked after the people.'

'Then why don't you ask Mr Franks-Walters to look after you now?' asked Annabel.

Mr Loader sighed. 'A gentleman like that must have such a lot on his plate,' he said. 'It wouldn't be fair to bother him with my troubles. Besides, even Mr Franks-Walters probably couldn't stand up against this lot.'

'What'll you do then?' asked Kate.

'I don't know,' he said. 'I suppose I'll have to look for somewhere else. But it's not easy. I've lived here all my life.'

Annabel and Kate left a few minutes later, each

carrying half a dozen fresh brown eggs that he'd given them.

'They just want to get rid of me, don't they,' he said, as they went off. 'They think I make Addendon untidy. I don't fit in.'

Annabel said little as she and Kate made their way homewards.

'Do you think there's anything we could do?' Kate asked at last. 'What about approaching Sheena and asking it she can get her father to help. Do you think she'd listen?'

'I've been wondering about that,' said Annabel.

'Even if we could get through to her, do you think it would do any good?'

'Dunno,' said Annabel. After a pause for further reflection, she said: 'I expect he's some kindly, well-meaning old stick. Perhaps he *would* have some advice on how to deal with these bye-laws and things. He must know the ropes if he was a Member of Parliament, mustn't he?'

'Anyway,' she added, 'there's no harm in having a try. We haven't got any other ideas and we've always wanted to find out about Sheena. Now's our chance!'

Annabel brightened up a little after that.

Thus it was that, for the sake of Mr Loader and his donkey, Eastbourne, Annabel and Kate set out to resolve the enigma of Sheena Franks-Walters.

Breaking the ice of Sheena's reserve turned out to be unexpectedly easy.

There happened to be a cross-country run on the Monday. The route was the usual circular one, winding up and around Addendon Hill and Beacon Hill.

Sheena Franks-Walters' style of cross-country running was to increase her pace marginally from her normal slow rate of walking to a moderate one, amiably bringing up the rear of the field, which was in any case not fast. Despite this, she was never too far behind at the finish and if there had been any known short-cut it would have been strongly suspected that she took it. However, if there were a short-cut through the dense scrub on the hills, no one else had succeeded in finding it.

On this occasion, for the first time ever, Sheena was not last in the field after the first quarter of a mile, Annabel and Kate having deliberately stayed behind her. They caught up with her on the bridle-path at the foot of Addendon Hill. She was standing rubbing her back violently against a gate-post.

'Anything the matter?' inquired Annabel, halting beside her.

'My back's itching all over,' said Sheena, continuing to squirm and wriggle up and down and from side to side with much feeling. 'I think someone's put some itching powder inside my games top.'

She gave them a dimpled, apologetic smile as if to convey her regret at the way she was making the scenery less attractive.

'The usual senseless practical joking,' said Annabel severely – she had herself applied the itching powder not long before – 'it never stops at Willers.'

'I didn't notice it at first,' said Sheena. 'Perhaps it's taken a little while to work its way through my vest.'

That had been Annabel's calculation exactly.

'I don't know quite what I'm going to do,' said Sheena, jerking up and down. 'It's getting worse.'

'It's very lucky,' said Annabel, 'but I always wear two games tops for cross-country running. I don't like getting cold. So perhaps if I were to give you one and you were to find somewhere to change . . .'

It had been Annabel's calculation that if she were to bring this situation about, helping Sheena out with a spare top – which she was now anxious to get rid of

28

anyway because it was too warm – so much goodwill and general bonhomie would be created by the process of changing tops and so on that the ice would be broken once and for all and a feeling of camaraderie established, making it possible to interrogate Sheena.

And certainly the plan appeared to be working to perfection. With many expressions of gratitude, Sheena disappeared hurriedly into some bushes with Annabel, who helpfully scratched her back until they got there. Kate stood and waited, patiently.

From behind the bushes came rustlings and stirrings, then various titters and squeakings. Annabel appeared to be brushing Sheena's back again and blowing on it – 'oooh! it's cold,' Kate heard Sheena giggle at one stage – before finally they emerged together, Sheena wearing Annabel's spare top and carrying her own and looking very cheerful.

' – it's so nice to be making friends at last,' she was saying. 'I've always wanted to but I must say I'd rather given up hope.'

'But we've always thought you wanted to keep to yourself,' said Annabel.

'Oh, no,' said Sheena. 'I didn't think anybody wanted to know *me*. Nobody ever says anything to me except to call me beastly names. Except for Julia Channing. I'm not sure about her. She comes up to me and says things like, "I think we people from more cultured backgrounds ought to stick together" and so on. I don't know whether she's joking or not. Anyway, I don't want to mix with people from cultured backgrounds. I want to mix with people like you.'

'Oh, thank you,' said Annabel. 'I – '

'My back's just got the teeniest itch still. I wonder if you could give it a little scratch . . . a little higher . . . thank you. Look, we must be terribly behind the others. But since we're friends now, I'll show you my

29

short-cut if you promise not to tell anybody. I had Blakey make it one weekend. I just couldn't possibly run all round that long course like the rest of you do. I always admire you so –'

'Blakey? Is –?'

'Our Head Gardener. He loved doing it, making me a secret way through all those prickly thorns and gorse bushes. He said it made him feel like a boy again. He leaves boxes of drinks and things half-way along so I can have a little picnic. I always enjoy cross-country running if it's a nice day. And now I've got someone to share it with it's just perfect.'

The ice had been broken. But would it be possible to staunch the resulting torrent long enough to carry out the interrogations and resolve the enigma?

Chapter 4

*****

The opportunity came over Sheena's drinks which she produced from under a fallen log half-way along her secret route. It was a very pleasant secret route and, as Sheena explained, brought you out at the bridle path coming down from Beacon Hill. It cut out about three-quarters of the cross-country run and the steepest parts at that.

There was only one glass and the bottles were large but, as Sheena said, it made it more friendly and intimate if they all took it in turns to drink from the same bottle. They sat on the log to do so.

Annabel had warmed considerably to Sheena, who clearly had hidden depths. While passing the bottle to her, Annabel took the opportunity of beginning the interrogation as casually as she could.

'What are you doing at Willers, anyway?' she asked. 'I mean, why do you stay at a crummy dump like this where they play stupid jokes and call you names? I'd have expected you to go to Roedean or somewhere.'

'Daddy wouldn't let me go to Roedean,' replied Sheena, lowering the bottle with satisfaction. 'Mummy went there, you see.'

'Oh,' said Annabel. She didn't quite follow. 'You mean – she told him Roedean's no good?'

'Oh, no,' said Sheena. 'I'm sure Roedean's an excellent school of its type. No, no. It's not that at all.

'You see, Daddy went to Eton and Oxford and so all

the rest of his life he's had to carry around this tremendous feeling of guilt at being privileged. He's determined that I shan't have to suffer in the same way. When I've left school I shall be able to feel superior to those girls who've been to Roedean and Cheltenham Ladies and so on. I shall be able to say modestly that I went to an ordinary state school called Lord Willoughby's and I've had to make my own way in the world.'

Annabel perked up. 'That's interesting,' she said. 'Does that mean that Kate and I will too, then?'

'Of course. In fact,' there was a note of regret in Sheena's voice as she passed the bottle to Kate, '– more than I shall because of course you'll have had the advantage of poor home backgrounds. You both live on some awful housing estate, don't you?'

'Yes,' said Annabel, smugly.

'It's no use my feeling jealous. It's just your good luck.'

'Does your mother feel the same way as your father?' asked Kate.

Sheena frowned. 'No. No, I'm not sure she does. She did say that he was a – but, anyway, I don't want to go into Mummy's faults. She tends to be a bit of an elitist and that's all there is to it. You can't entirely shake off your upbringing, I suppose.'

'No,' said Annabel, sympathetically.

'Don't you think we ought to be going?' asked Kate.

'We have to get the timing right,' said Sheena, looking cautiously at her tiny gold watch. 'One has to be very careful not to walk in first in the cross-country. It would look suspicious.'

'You're right,' said Annabel, still further impressed by this example of foresight and planning, proof that things actually went on inside Sheena's head.

'Still,' continued Sheena, 'I think it's all right now. Just about right, in fact.'

They proceeded in single file, Sheena in the lead.

'What would be rather nice, now that I've got to know you better', she said a little shyly, after they had gone a short distance, 'is – but perhaps it's rather a cheek to push myself forward like this –'

'Go on,' said Annabel, handsomely.

'– is if you'd let me – I wonder if you could give me just a teeny scratch again – thank you – if you'd let me come to tea with both of you sometimes. It would be very useful experience. You see, I never go into ordinary homes. Mummy and Daddy and I live in this terrible great place. It's so huge and it's got all these stables and swimming pools and things so we've got this feeling of shame all the time about living there – at least, Daddy and I have. I'm not sure about Mummy.'

'Can't you move to somewhere smaller?' asked Annabel, sympathetically.

'If only we could,' said Sheena, then she lapsed into silence. Then she continued: 'And when we go and visit any of Daddy's friends their houses are much the same as ours, you see. Daddy's friends tend to be very privileged, politicians and people like that, mostly . . .'

'Are they suffering, too?' asked Annabel.

'Daddy says the more thoughtful and compassionate ones are. Some just live it up and have a good time and don't care about anybody else. He tries to avoid those if he can . . .

'So you see how it is. Do you know, I quite frequently go for walks round the poorer parts of Addendon on winter evenings and try to peer into houses through the cracks in the curtains. Just to try to find out how the common people live when they're at home.'

'What do you see?' asked Kate.

Sheena frowned. 'Television sets flickering,

mostly. I long to be able to pull the curtains back and see what's happening in the rest of the room.'

'Someone sleeping in an armchair, perhaps?' suggested Annabel.

'I want to find out about what Daddy calls – oh, look, perhaps I shouldn't be talking this way, making you feel as if I'm putting you under some sort of microscope. I normally don't breathe a word about my opinions but we seem to be getting on so well together –'

'Oh, we are,' said Annabel. 'And we don't mind at all, do we, Kate. We're interested.'

'Good,' said Sheena, with relief. 'Just for a moment I – but, anyway, I want to find what Daddy calls "the throbbing vital soul of the working classes".'

Annabel looked dubious. 'I was going to suggest you had a peek through our curtains,' she said, 'but you seem to be expecting rather a lot . . . what about your house, Kate?'

'It would have to be a very lucky evening for you to see anything like that,' said Kate.

'Anyway,' said Annabel, 'you're welcome to come to tea any time. It'll be warmer than peeking through the curtains.'

'Same here,' said Kate.

'Thank you,' said Sheena.

'There's just one thing,' said Annabel. 'Any chance of – er – of a return match?'

Sheena looked blank. 'You don't mean,' she said, cottoning on after a time, 'coming to tea with *us*.'

'Well,' said Annabel, 'er –'

'But –' Sheena looked baffled. 'Of course. Though I can't quite see why you want to. I'm quite flattered really. There's nothing much to see at our house.'

'We could look at the swimming pool,' suggested Annabel. 'Even try it out, perhaps.'

A dimpled smile dawned slowly upon Sheena's

face. 'I'm being silly, aren't I,' she said. 'Of course you'd like to see how other people live, too. It's perfectly natural. Just because a way of life seems so boring to me, it doesn't mean it's not without interest to someone like you ... I'm rather unimaginative, aren't I.'

'Not at all,' said Annabel.

'So should we fix up these visits now?' asked Sheena. 'Oh, no ... that would be much too formal, wouldn't it. You working-class people don't go in for all the formal nonsense that we do. I must say I'm a bit of a rebel about it, although one has to bow to convention some of the time. As I was saying, you can't entirely escape your upbringing, can you.'

'Unfortunately, no,' said Annabel.

'One thing I do make a stand about, though,' said Sheena, with sudden vehemence, '*and* I'm a total rebel here, I'm afraid *and* I don't care who knows it. When I go visiting I never, *ever* tip the servants and when you come to our house I'd advise you not to do so, either.'

'We won't,' promised Annabel, 'will we, Kate. Just one thing, though. I don't want to be too formal but what about tomorrow?'

'To visit? Well, yes, that'll be lovely. I'll let Cook know. You can come back with me in the car after school.'

'We'll look forward to that,' said Annabel, 'won't we, Kate.'

'Do you think we're arriving at the other bridle-path?' asked Kate. She thought she had heard a faint cough somewhere ahead.

'Yes,' said Sheena. 'We have to be a tiny bit cautious here.'

Following her example, Annabel and Kate halted and peered between two thorn bushes. On the other side of them lay the bridle-path.

A figure was lounging along it, about to disappear from view round a bend. That slinky back was unmistakeable. They didn't need the further evidence of the puff of blue smoke that floated over the right shoulder and another faint choking cough to tell them who it was.

'Justine Bird,' said Kate.

'What perfect timing!' said Sheena, with satisfaction. 'I know when I see Justine go by that there can't be anybody else behind her. We're safe.'

'Well,' whispered Kate afterwards as they changed, 'what do you make of all that? Have we resolved anything?'

Annabel was frowning.

'I don't know, Kate,' she said. 'We got an earful but I've a feeling we're just scratching the surface.'

'Anyway, what about Mr Loader? That's the urgent thing.'

'Oh, we've made a big advance there, haven't we. We've got an invitation to Addendon Court. We shall be able to sum up Mr Franks-Walters and see if he might be able to help. If Sheena lets us get a word in, that is.

'Anyway,' she added, 'he sounds very well-meaning, doesn't he. At least his heart seems to be in the right place.'

Chapter 5

*****

That afternoon Annabel tried, as a rather desperate second string, to contact the Hackney and Wester Ross Property Company just in case they might relent and let Mr Loader have his grazing land back. She got the telephone number by ringing Hazelford's, the estate agents, and pretending she was the secretary of someone who wanted to do business with them.

'The Hackney and Wester Ross?' said the girl at the other end of the line. 'I don't know anything about them, I'm afraid. I'll have to fetch Mr Clark.'

'What sort of business does your company want to do with them?' Mr Clark wanted to know.

'Important business,' replied Annabel.

'Is it about the plot of land with the frontage on to Stumbury, perhaps, er –' It sounded as if he were riffling through some papers –

'Yes, that's it,' said Annabel. 'Our company's got a proposition to put to them.'

'Oh,' he said, 'I don't think they'll be very interested. I think they may have some project under way already. I don't really know much about it. In fact we don't really have much to do with them – look, perhaps I should speak to your boss –'

'Oh, Mr Eastbourne would be very cross if he had to deal with something as trivial as this,' said Annabel. 'I only want the number.'

'We don't ever really have any reason to call them,'

said Mr Clark apologetically. 'But here it is, I think, yes . . . it's a London number . . .'

Mr Bunce wouldn't have been very pleased to know that she was dialling London but it was in an excellent cause.

Some time elapsed before anyone answered. Then:

'Oo's that?' said a voice at the other end. This was followed by some raucous coughing and the sound of a nose being blown.

'Good afternoon,' said Annabel, in her most responsible voice. 'Is that the Hackney and Wester Ross Property Company?'

The response was a guffaw which went on for some time. Then the voice said to someone else: 'She wants to know if it's the Hackney and Wester Ross Property Company.' There were other guffaws. 'No love,' said the voice. 'It's not.'

'Then what is it?' asked Annabel, her voice reverting to normal.

'It's a building site off the Mile End Road. An old shed. They calls it the site office.'

But it was the right number. 'Funny company!' frowned Annabel as she put the phone down. She sighed. 'Oh, well. That's no good. It was a long shot, anyway.'

Afterwards, Annabel and Kate called to see Mr Loader and Eastbourne for a few minutes.

'A lady who runs a home for retired donkeys called today,' said Mr Loader. 'She offered to take Eastbourne. Mrs Stringer put her on to me, so she said.'

'So what happened?' asked Annabel. 'Is he going there?'

'No,' said Mr Loader. 'Eastbourne knocked her over. She did go on a bit,' he added as an afterthought.

'We could have guessed, couldn't we, Kate,' said Annabel. 'Eastbourne's got good taste.'

She gave him a pat.

'Still, perhaps I should have taken up the offer,' said Mr Loader. 'It'd be terrible but what else is there? I don't know what I'm going to do.'

On the following afternoon, Annabel and Kate accompanied Sheena to the waiting vintage limousine. It was a pleasant day and the hood was down. They were watched by an interested audience and the look on Julia Channing's face alone would have made it all worthwhile.

'I hope you've had a pleasant, day, Miss Sheena,' said the chauffeur as he held the door open for them.

'Thank you, Bennion,' said Sheena. 'I'm bringing some friends home with me today.'

A ball of rolled-up paper hit Annabel on the head just as the car started to move away. She looked around sharply and made as if to throw it back but she couldn't identify the culprit. There were several possibilities. So she dropped it on the floor instead.

'I've never had any friends come back with me before,' said Sheena complacently. 'It's quite exciting. Mummy and Daddy were quite surprised.'

Annabel and Kate concentrated on savouring the drive, Annabel giving patronizing nods to motorists who eyed the car with interest or envy. To get to Addendon Court you have to travel out of Addendon along the Cogginton Road for about five minutes, then turn left.

'What does your father do?' Annabel asked Sheena after she had got over the first thrill. 'Does he have to work?'

'Oh, of course,' replied Sheena. 'We're not like those revolting people who live on inherited wealth. At least we're not as bad as that. Granny did leave quite a bit, of course, a few hundred thousand, I think, but that soon went, what was left after taxes, and then my other gramps did leave us the house and a few bits and pieces of furniture. But otherwise nothing. No, my father lives by his wits.'

'By his wits?'

'Yes, it's demeaning, isn't it. But then beggars can't be choosers. Mind you he was a Member of Parliament for a time and that's supposed to be quite respectable, isn't it. He was even Parliamentary Secretary to the Minister of Drains or something or other. But he had to resign. On principle.'

'What was the principle?' asked Kate.

Sheena tittered, her shoulders shaking a little.

'He always says the principle was that he shouldn't be found out. Though that's only a joke, of course. You mustn't go repeating it. It's naughty of me to tell you. You might get the wrong idea.'

'Found out about what?' asked Annabel.

'There you are, you see? Just when I said it was a little joke. Let's talk about you instead, should we?'

The car turned left off the Cogginton Road into a smaller road. There was a little signpost saying *Addendon Court*.

'I expect both *your* fathers do something socially useful, don't they,' said Sheena, looking at Annabel and Kate. 'And your mothers too, I'll bet. I'm afraid my mother doesn't' – Sheena's face clouded over as it usually seemed to when she spoke of her mother – 'I must confess she spends all her time enjoying herself. She says she can't see what's liberated about trailing off to an office every day and being bossed around by somebody. I do try to make her see reason but I'm afraid it's an uphill task.'

She looked at Annabel and Kate expectantly.

'My father works in the office at Beldews,' said Kate. 'That's a factory on the industrial estate,' she added.

'I've seen their name in the local paper,' said Sheena. 'They often advertise for staff, don't they. What do they make?'

'Come to think of it,' said Kate, 'I don't know. It's something electronic, isn't it, Annabel?'

'I don't know either,' said Annabel. 'I've never thought about it. But they must make something or there wouldn't be any point in having a factory.'

'Quite,' said Sheena. 'They obviously have a product and whatever it is your father helps them to make it or get rid of it or something. So there you are, you see. You're one up on me as usual.'

'I don't think I am,' said Annabel, who was feeling sorry for Sheena and anxious to make her feel better. 'My father works in local government.'

Annabel and Kate were distracted by the fact of the car turning under a magnificent stone archway which formed the entrance to the grounds of Addendon Court. Beyond lay a vision of splendour unimagined in Badger's Close and Oakwood Crescent.

The grounds of Addendon Court spread as far as the eye could see. A vast expanse of parkland, shaded by cedar and pine, was interspersed with shrubberies and rose gardens. In the distance, a herd of deer grazed by a lake (a lake which was known to Mr Loader like the back of his hand and from which he drew his Friday trout). Somewhere, as if to emphasize the silence of the limousine's engine, a motor mower made a soothing, purring sound.

Across this idyllic expanse the limousine sailed, on a white-paved drive the width of a motorway and flanked by stone urns and statues of various Greek gods and goddesses and by many rare and exotic trees and shrubs.

Ahead, dramatic on the horizon, stood its goal, the house itself, turreted and bespired.

'Like a fairy castle!' murmured Annabel. 'Fit for an enchanted princess.'

Beside her, the resident princess tittered plumply.

'I suppose I don't quite live up to that, do I?' said Sheena complacently.

'We are here on a quest,' Annabel murmured to herself. 'Like the knights of old.'

'A what?' inquired Sheena, baffled, only half-hearing.

'Nothing,' replied Annabel, rousing herself. She nodded at the house. 'Fourteenth century?' she hazarded.

'1882,' replied Sheena. 'It gets burnt down about once a century and they keep on rebuilding it. Apparently it gets dafter each time.' She tittered again.

As the limousine rolled to a halt outside the subject under discussion, Kate was reflecting upon three things. They were: One – perhaps, after all, Mr Franks-Walters didn't sound quite like the kindly old stick that she and Annabel had imagined. A re-think seemed necessary.

Two – had Annabel met her match at talking? Now that Sheena Franks-Walters had started, was she ever going to stop?

Three – were they getting anywhere with their quest?

'Just tell me what you'd like to do,' said Sheena as they entered the house through one of its smaller doors at the rear. 'Whether you'd like to swim or play croquet or go riding or what. This is my treat. We'll have some tea and look over the house first, of course, if that's what you want to do. You'll have to tell me though because I don't know. It all seems a frantic bore to me.'

'On a day like this, a swim, I think,' said Annabel.

'Outdoor or indoor pool?'

'Outdoor. And if we could meet your parents –'

'Oh, of course. They're dying to meet you. We'll do that first.'

Sheena led the way through various corridors. 'I expect they're in the afternoon drawing-room,' she said, pushing open a door. 'Oh, yes. There's Daddy.'

Some distance away, in the centre of the room, a man was seated in a high-backed armchair which was covered in some gold-coloured material. He was surveying a pink-coloured newspaper which lay on a walnut coffee table in front of him.

He was a large, hearty-looking man with hair that was starting to recede. The stub of a cigar protruded from one side of his mouth. There were large holes in the elbows of his sagging old dark green sweater and his shirt sleeves hung through them.

'Daddy,' said Sheena, 'I'd like you to meet my friends, Annabel Bunce and Kate Stocks.'

'Nice to meet you,' he said, taking the cigar from his mouth. 'Good to see that Sheena's so popular. Miserable place this, though, don't you think? Dreary. No neighbours. Never see anybody from morning till night except the servants. And my wife, of course. Got to travel a long way before you can find somebody worth talking to. Where do you two live?'

'Daddy, you are a silly old forgetter,' said Sheena. 'I told you. On one of those estates in Addendon.'

'Oh,' he said, looking at them with interest. 'Yes. I was saying to Sheena how much I envy people like you. Be quite different where you live. So much neighbourliness. The women sitting on their doorsteps in the sunshine, gossiping to each other across the street –'

'Oh, Daddy, it's not like that at all,' said Sheena, laughing. 'You're such a silly. I've been there and had a look.'

He sighed. 'Isn't it? Oh, I suppose television's killing all that sort of thing off. No, I expect one has to go to the north now for real friendliness.'

He looked wistful.

'Do you know what I'd like to be able to do?' he said. 'I'd like to throw all this lot aside – give it all away – and go and live in a mining village and be a miner. Hard physical toil all day but plenty of good fellowship, then home in the evening to the cosy fire and the little wife.' He sighed again.

'Can't you do that?' asked Annabel.

'If only I could,' he said, and lapsed into silence.

Annabel thought he must have disposed of her question for he said nothing more for a few moments. Then he added, sadly:

'Someone's got to keep the wheels turning. One has to be around to do one's duty and see that the great mass of the people are decently housed and cared for, even if it does mean some sacrifices. One can't just throw aside one's responsibilities, you know.'

The thought seemed to move him deeply and he allowed his chin to sink into his chest while he savoured it.

In the ensuing brief silence, Kate noticed that Annabel was picking up a piece of paper from a very large ashtray which lay on the coffee table.

The paper was charred and had evidently been used as a taper for lighting a pipe. Other, similarly charred pieces of paper lay in the ashtray and a pipe lay beside it.

Kate noticed that in the huge fireplace there was a jar of such tapers, formed from folded pieces of paper.

Annabel had retained the paper and was now holding it in her hand. Kate couldn't imagine why.

The door opened and a tall, languid butler appeared.

'What do you want, Percival?' Mr Franks-Walters asked, emerging from his self-pity.

'I rang for him,' said a voice in an even more distant part of the room. It came from an armchair by the french windows which, because the high back was turned towards them, Kate hadn't realized was occupied. Now a hand and arm, a glass held in the hand, appeared from behind it. Then a head emerged, too. It was a very glamorous head with a great deal of golden hair.

'I'd like another of these, Percival,' she said, 'and this time less of the soda water.'

The butler took the glass and went out. The head disappeared again.

'That's Mummy,' said Sheena. 'Hallo, Mummy. Annabel and Kate are here.' She made a sort of shocked, tut-tutting face at her father as if to say 'there she goes, letting us down again'.

'Pleased to meet you,' said the voice. 'I heard my husband boring you with his talk about mining villages. He tells everybody that. Don't pay any attention to him. He'd fall down in a faint if they showed him a real pithead.'

Sheena clicked her tongue and gave a furious little toss of the head.

'And if he thinks I'm going to be the cosy little wife,' continued the voice, 'he's got another think coming. He's mean enough as it is, using old envelopes twice and all the other things he gets up to. I already have to fight and struggle for every mink coat.'

'I think it's time we had some tea,' Sheena said stiffly to Annabel and Kate. 'See you later, Daddy.'

Some time later, Annabel and Kate lay by the swimming pool. They had splashed in the pool but only briefly because, as Annabel said, it probably wasn't wise to do a *lot* of swimming after so much clotted cream and strawberry flan and other things (Mr Franks-Walters' economies not extending, on the evidence they had seen, to the Addendon Court food supplies).

Sheena plodded off in pursuit of more apple juice.

'You didn't ask Mr Franks-Walters whether he could help about Mr Loader, did you, Annabel,' observed Kate, when she'd gone.

'No,' said Annabel. She got up and, having glanced round to make sure that Sheena wasn't returning, nipped into a changing cubicle and returned with a crumpled scrap of paper with burnt edges which she passed to Kate. It was the scrap of paper she had retrieved from the ashtray.

Kate smoothed it out. It had originally been a sheet of headed notepaper. Only the top part had been left unburned and on this was printed

CKNEY AND WESTER ROSS PROP

Beneath it was a London address and a familiar telephone number.

'Hackney and Wester Ross Property Company!' exclaimed Kate, sitting up. 'What a coincidence!'

She pondered.

'Was this a letter to Mr Franks-Walters from the company or – ?'

'There seemed to be a lot of other sheets just the same,' said Annabel. 'Blank ones.'

'You mean he might *be* the Hackney and Wester Ross? But that'd be amazing.'

'Yes, it's funny, isn't it,' Annabel agreed. 'That's why I didn't say anything. I thought we ought to think a bit more first.'

'But . . .' said Kate '. . . if he is, it might be marvellous. He might let Mr Loader have his grazing back.'

'I'm going for another swim,' said Annabel.

There was a splash as she dived in.

Kate felt a little hurt at the way Annabel had ignored her remark. It hadn't been as daft as all that. Had it?

Chapter 6

*****

'I hope you haven't been too frantically bored,' said Sheena.

'Not at all,' said Annabel.

'We've had a lovely time,' said Kate.

They were about to leave. Annabel was carrying a large slice of chocolate gateau, wrapped in a napkin, pressed upon her by Sheena after she had coveted it.

'I mean, you're sure there isn't anything else you'd like to see while you're here,' said Sheena. 'You'll have to tell me if there is, I'm afraid, because as I said the whole boiling seems boring to me.'

'What it would be nice to see –' began Annabel. Then she paused. 'But perhaps it's rather a cheek.'

'It can't be more of a cheek than the things I say to you,' said Sheena. 'Go on.'

'I'd be quite interested to see where your father works. Does he have a study or something like that?'

'That *is* a funny thing to want to see,' said Sheena, wonderingly. 'But then I suppose some of the things I want to see sound funny to you. Well, if that really appeals, I don't suppose Daddy would mind. It's a bit of a trudge, though. It's in the west wing.'

Mr Franks-Walters' study did look, on the face of it, uninteresting. It was a large room with an antique desk in the middle, book-shelves and ancestral portraits along the walls and a row of filing cabinets. The desk was covered with papers.

Annabel however seemed to find the room full of interest, wandering round examining things closely and exclaiming how fascinating it was actually to see the inner sanctum of a great man like Mr Franks-Walters and how it quite sent goose-pimples down her spine, remarks which caused Sheena to titter wonderingly.

Even when she had been all round the room, Annabel appeared reluctant to leave. Then Sheena noticed that some of the chocolate in her gateau was melting.

'I really ought to have put that in a bag!' said Sheena. 'I wonder if there's an envelope or something – oh, look! Here's one.' She bent down and produced a large envelope from a waste-paper basket.

'Put it in there,' she said. 'You don't mind about it being in the waste bin, do you? It's very clean.'

'Not at all,' said Annabel, 'but –' she peered into the envelope. 'There's something inside. A photograph.'

She took the photograph out and they all looked at it. It was a colour picture of a small, bald-headed man and, beside him, a square-shaped woman, presumably husband and wife. In front of the couple were four children of various shapes and sizes. They were all in swimwear and behind them were some coconut palms and what appeared to be the terrace of a very luxurious hotel.

Scrawled across the bottom of the picture were the words:

From Bert (the Drain!) and all the family in Hawaii. Just to show you how much we're enjoying ourselves and many thanks.
    P.S. Burn this picture! Ha ha!

'What a strange picture,' said Sheena. 'Daddy has

49

some really quite extraordinary friends, you know. You should see some of the people who've been to our house. Quite uncultivated, many of them. But that's why I admire him so much, I suppose. He's such a socially caring person. He has the common touch, the touch', she continued, in a more declamatory style, 'that can mix with commoners and royalty and treat both of them just the same. Is that Kipling? It sounds like Kipling, doesn't it. But perhaps it isn't. Perhaps I've just made it up myself.'

She made to throw the picture back into the waste-paper basket but Annabel restrained her.

'I'd like that if you haven't got any use for it,' she said. 'It's just what I need to finish off my lampshade.'

'Your lampshade?' inquired Sheena.

'I'm making one covered with coloured photos. Hawaii would be really perfect to finish it off.'

'Oh, of course, if you want it,' said Sheena. 'After all, it says it's to be burnt so obviously nobody wants it any longer.'

Annabel had an air of triumph about her as Bennion drove them away.

'I hope you found your visit worthwhile,' called Sheena, waving them off.

'Even more than I expected,' replied Annabel, graciously. 'You must return the visit, mustn't she, Kate.'

'I'm just waiting for the invitation,' called Sheena.

Despite the air of triumph, Annabel didn't seem anxious to talk as they drove away. Perhaps she was worried in case Bennion would overhear. Perhaps she just wanted to think.

'What do you make of the picture?' asked Kate, keeping her voice low.

'It's interesting, isn't it,' murmured Annabel.

'You've given up any idea of asking Mr Franks-Walters if he can help about Eastbourne?'

'Oh, I wouldn't say that, Kate. No, I think we may well ask him. But not yet. Soon. Let's think about it a bit more.'

'What about the enigma?' asked Kate, as Annabel showed signs of retreating into silence again. 'Are we getting anywhere with that?'

'We are making progress,' replied Annabel, snuggling more deeply into the seat. They drove into Addendon in silence.

As the limousine was drawing up at the end of Oakwood Crescent, Annabel said suddenly: 'If I call for you in about ten minutes' time, will you come and visit Mrs Stringer with me? I think we ought to have a chat with her.'

'Mrs Stringer!' repeated Kate, in some astonishment.

'I'd like to ask her about the history of Addendon. She knows all about it.'

'Well, if you think –'

The limousine had halted and Bennion was opening the door. It was time to be pitched back into the real world. At Badger's Close, Annabel was pitched back, too. It was hard.

A short while later, Annabel and Kate rang the bell at Mrs Stringer's house in Mill Lane.

'Goodness gracious!' said that august windbag, startled but gratified when Annabel told her why they'd called. Mrs Stringer had past cause for not feeling warmly disposed towards Annabel but a request such as this wiped out unpleasant memories. Perhaps she had misjudged the girl.

'I shall show you my slides,' she said. 'Come this way.'

She led them past the open door to the sitting-room – through which could be glimpsed, reading a newspaper, the elderly gentleman who was presumably

Mr Stringer – and into another room, with a desk in it, her study.

Here she produced her slides, slide projector and screen.

'Please sit down,' she said. 'I should like you to see something of Addendon as it was before it was developed over the last few years. I've tried to make some sort of pictorial record of it.'

Annabel and Kate sat side by side and watched old Addendon unfold before them. Thatched cottages, leafy corners, mellow old walls. Much of it remained but much too had disappeared.

'This was my favourite,' said Mrs Stringer, 'the Goosemarket. All pulled down now, I'm afraid.'

She had several slides of the Goosemarket. Rows of medieval houses, their upper storeys bulging, surrounded an irregular patch of green upon which a flock of geese were grazing.

'There wasn't a market there,' said Mrs Stringer, 'though I suppose there might once have been. But there was a common right for people to graze their geese and poultry there. There was a lovely bank of primroses in the spring, too.

'I used to walk around there on Sunday mornings. The atmosphere was so lovely and right in the town, too. You don't seem to find that atmosphere any more.' She sighed.

'They pulled that down!' said Kate. 'But why? It was lovely!'

'It was, wasn't it,' said Mrs Stringer. 'It was very beautiful. I love Addendon but so much of it has been destroyed and brutalized. Since then, I have immersed myself in trying to help others. I have swallowed my own feelings and tried to welcome the newcomers into the community. What else could I do? I –'

'Where was the Goosemarket?' asked Annabel, stopping the flow.

'Oddly enough,' said Mrs Stringer, 'you are probably living on the site. You live in – er –?'

'Badger's Close. Kate lives in Oakwood Crescent.'

'Yes, well the Goosemarket was demolished in order to facilitate the building of that estate. It was very unfortunate, I tried to get a preservation order on it but the bulldozers beat me to it, I'm afraid. It is very unfortunate that Mr Franks-Walters happened to be away that weekend –'

'Mr Franks-Walters?'

'He did own the Goosemarket originally but unfortunately he was talked into selling it to some property company. They assured him that they would never pull it down and they wished to buy it only to refurbish it and keep the houses in good repair ... such a good, trusting man, Mr Franks-Walters. While all the time they were applying for planning permission without his knowledge.'

'But what company was it?' asked Kate.

'Oh, I can't remember. It was very complicated, you know. That company was owned by another company which was in turn owned by yet another. And so on. It was very difficult to find out who was actually behind it all. There was a sort of fever at the time, you see. Like a gold rush. There were big profits to be made out of land and building and developing Addendon. I always had the feeling, though, that there was a lot of manipulation going on, that there was some mastermind behind it all.'

'A Mr Big,' said Annabel.

'I suppose you could say that. Mr Franks-Walters and I fought against it but we were not powerful enough.' She sighed. 'It was the main drainage being brought to Addendon that did it, I'm afraid. If it hadn't been for that . . .'

'Drains!' said Annabel.

'Yes. It was all very unfortunate and rather mysterious. I had been told that Addendon wasn't on the list for getting main drainage. Then suddenly it happened and Addendon became ripe for development.'

'Drains,' said Annabel again.

She and Kate looked at each other.

'Drains!' whispered Kate. *The old crook!*

'It has been a comfort to talk to you,' said Mrs Stringer as they left.

'Mrs Stringer,' said Annabel. 'I wonder if you know what's going on with that bit of land on Stumbury, the open space next to the Smithy?'

A strange look crossed Mrs Stringer's face, a look compounded of fury and obstinacy.

'That is a sore subject with the Town Council,' she said. 'We believe that there are various machinations going on.'

'Machinations?'

'We believe that there is a planning application in with the District Council to build a shopping centre there and that the Town Council is being deliberately kept out of it. I don't want to say too much but it is something I am trying to take up with Mr Franks-Walters. I think we need his help and influence once again in fighting it.'

'He wasn't much help before,' said Annabel.

Mrs Stringer regarded her sternly.

'He did all he could. I will not hear a word against Mr Franks-Walters. He is a fine man, a man of the people. I also consider myself – I hope I am not being presumptuous here – to be a friend of his in a small way. On several occasions I have had the honour, the *great* honour, I might say, of being entertained at Addendon Court.'

*

54

'Daddy's rather cross with me,' said Sheena next day at lunch time. 'He says I shouldn't have given you that photograph. I told him that he's being a silly, he'd thrown it away, but he said that was a mistake. He's wondering if you could let him have it back again.'

'Oh dear!' said Annabel. 'I've stuck it on my lamp-shade now. It'll ruin it if I take it off.'

Sheena looked nonplussed and, to take the strain off her mind, selected another sandwich.

'Still, I will do that if it means such a lot to him,' said Annabel. 'I wonder, though, if you could ask your father to do something for me. There's a Mr Loader who lives in the Smithy on the corner of Stumbury and Gamble Street. He's got a donkey but nowhere to graze it and there's a lovely piece of land right next to him owned by the Hackney and Wester Ross Property Company. I wondered if your father might try and use his influence with them to see if Mr Loader can graze Eastbourne there.'

'I'd better make a note of that,' said Sheena, producing a diary and gold-topped pen from her pocket. 'What did you say the donkey's name was?'

'Eastbourne,' said Annabel. 'E-A-S-T-B-O-U-R-N-E.'

'Did you ask your father?' inquired Annabel, next day.

'He doesn't really think there's anything he can do,' said Sheena. 'He'd love to help, of course, that goes without saying but . . . well, he just doesn't have any influence. Did you bring the picture?'

'Oh dear!' exclaimed Annabel, snapping her fingers. 'How awful of me! I forgot. Perhaps you could ask your father again tonight. I don't want to be a nuisance but it is important.'

*

'He really doesn't have any influence,' said Sheena, plaintively, on the following morning. 'He only wishes he had. Did you bring the picture?'

'Oh, aren't I a *silly*,' said Annabel. 'Brain like a sieve.'

Sheena looked fretful. 'Daddy's getting so touchy about it and seems to think it's all my fault. He says the picture is of great sentimental value to him because that Bert Drain person was a very dear friend of his and so was Mrs Drain or whatever her name was and the Drain children. They were all very dear to him and now I've given their picture away. He says it must have fallen into the waste-paper basket accidentally because he certainly never intended to get rid of it. He just took it out of a drawer to look at and think fondly about Bert and all the good times they've had together.

'That's what he says,' continued Sheena, a slight note of pettishness entering her tone, 'but I think Daddy's a bit of an old hindsighter if you ask me. I'd never heard of this Bert person before. Still,' she continued, cheering up a little, 'it can't be helped. Look, about this visit. I don't want to push but I happened to mention it to Daddy and he thought it was a lovely idea and he'd like to come too if it wouldn't be too much trouble. In fact it was the only thing that seemed to put him into a better mood. He'd specially like to come to your house, Annabel, because he's always particularly liked the sound of Badger's Close. He's always thought it such a lovely name for a street and he's just thrilled at the thought of actually visiting it.'

'Well, that would be a great privilege, of course,' replied Annabel. 'Your father coming to honour our little house in Badger's Close. Provided that Kate doesn't mind me having all the glory. I mean I'm sure you'd like Sheena's father to visit Oakwood Crescent, wouldn't you, Kate.'

'We can do that some other time,' said Sheena. 'You wouldn't have thought Daddy would be such an old sentimentalizer, would you?'

'No,' said Annabel. 'I'll speak to Mum about it and ask her when the best time is. I'm looking forward to it.'

Chapter 7

*****

The news of the proposed visit by the Franks-Walters threw the Bunce household into a state of confusion. Mr Bunce said that they'd better be invited while he was out at work because he had no idea what to talk to Mr Franks-Walters about.

Mrs Bunce was petrified, saying that she didn't have any idea what to talk about either but she had no choice. She had to be there.

Annabel said that if her mother would only fix a day, she'd tell Sheena when she saw her at school but Mrs Bunce got into a still bigger flap and said they couldn't behave like that, what would the Franks-Walters think of them? No, they had to do things properly and formally. She was uninterested when Annabel assured her that Sheena expected informality and would be disappointed if she didn't get it.

Annabel's attitude was that they should try to give Sheena value for money and real thrills by messing the place up and making it look as slummy as possible. She suggested that her mother might contribute to this by, for example, putting on her oldest clothes and sitting slumped on the floor in the corner of the sitting-room, drinking and smoking a pipe. She felt that Sheena would be disappointed by anything less.

Mrs Bunce rejected this indignantly. Instead, she dashed out and caught the newsagents before they closed. There she purchased an invitation card, hovering indecisively for some time over two, one of which bore the message *request the pleasure of the company of* and the other *at home*, before finally choosing the latter. She also bought a book on etiquette and a little cookery book entitled *That Special Guest*.

The invitation was dispatched by the 6 o'clock post. It read:

> *Mrs Bunce and Annabel*
> *AT HOME*
> *to Mr and Mrs Franks-Walters and Sheena*
> *4.30 p.m. Wednesday*
> *R.S.V.P. 9 Badger's Close*

Mrs Bunce explained that she had to invite Mrs Franks-Walters out of courtesy although, of course, she wouldn't be coming. 'I can't understand why *Mr* Franks-Walters wants to come anyway,' she said, wonderingly. 'Can you understand it, Annabel?'

'Yes, Mum,' said Annabel, her thoughts going to that lampshade up in her room decorated with coloured photos. 'Yes, I understand it all right.'

It was the Friday evening.

On Sunday morning, Sheena rang up. Annabel was with Kate in the garden when her mother called her in to the phone.

'Of course we'd love to come, I don't know why you had to waste money on that card,' said Sheena. 'Mummy keeps on saying how much she's looking forward to it.'

'Your mother's coming?' said Annabel.

'Oh, yes. Dying to. So you can see how much Daddy and I want to.'

The news threw Mrs Bunce into a still greater state of agitation. To her, Mrs Franks-Walters was a remote and fearsome figure, glimpsed occasionally sitting magisterially under the dryer at the *Smart Set*, fussed around by Fabian and his entire staff, while lesser mortals like Mrs Bunce sat patient and forgotten. Or presenting prizes on some distant platform: or wandering about at point-to-points with a shooting stick and field glasses. The thought that this being from another planet should materialize in her sitting-room waiting to be fed was petrifying. Mrs Bunce returned feverishly to her book of etiquette and *That Special Guest*, wondering how she could compete with the cook at Addenton Hall.

The only consolation, she explained to Annabel, was that it was so nice to see that her daughter was mixing in such socially desirable circles. Not merely nice, she implied by her tone of voice, but awe-inspiring. Her daughter, commented Mrs Bunce, a hint of pride in her voice, must have something special.

'Yes, Mum, I have,' replied Annabel, thinking of the lampshade again. She went slowly out into the garden where Kate was waiting for her and her father was digging, with the transistor radio playing softly.

'They're coming?' asked Kate as Annabel joined her.

'*All* of them,' nodded Annabel in reply. But she seemed abstracted. She appeared to be listening to the music.

'*All* of them?' repeated Kate, in astonishment. 'Mrs Franks-Walters as well?'

Annabel nodded again. 'Hang on a minute,' she said and to Kate it seemed as if there were a catch in her voice.

Annabel walked over to the radio and turned up the volume and as the music swelled out she straightened up and stood motionless listening to it. Kate wondered if she were about to burst into tears.

This was quite possible because Annabel was capable of becoming very emotional about music – and this was certainly very lovely music. It was a fairly frequent source of embarrassment to Kate. When they had gone to *Madame Butterfly* together, Annabel had sobbed and wailed all through the performance, being hushed and hissed and glared at by people until a particularly hysterical outburst had almost thrown the soprano out of her stride during her aria and Annabel had been offered her money back by the manager.

'What's that music?' Annabel asked of her father now. He had finished digging and was pushing the earth off his spade with the toe of his boot.

'Vaughan Williams,' he said. 'Fantasia on a Theme by Thomas Tallis.'

'There's Addendon as it used to be in that music,' said Annabel, and there was a definite break in her voice now. 'The Goosemarket and the primrose bank and the village green and no television aerials . . . England as it was.'

The music swelled out into the garden, complementing the blue sky and the sunshine and the white clouds and the brown earth on Mr Bunce's boots and the bits of green hedges that grew between the backs of the houses.

'England before Mr Franks-Walters got at it,' said Annabel. 'He was one of the people who were in charge of it, who were supposed to be looking after it.'

'Better turn the radio down at bit,' said Mr Bunce. 'It might be disturbing the neighbours.'

The music was coming to an end anyway as he lowered the volume and, picking up the radio, he carried it inside the house, enabling them to hear some heavy rock music emanating from a transistor radio in the garden of a house two doors along where the Atkins were sitting out in deckchairs on their concrete patio.

'Come on, Kate. Let's go for a walk,' said Annabel. She was brushing away a tear.

They went out through the house and into Badger's Close. As the gate swung to behind them, Annabel paused and said: 'The enigma of Sheena Franks-Walters is starting to fit into place, Kate.'

'Is it?' said Kate.

'Yes,' said Annabel. 'It's a startling story of . . .' she rolled her eyes . . . 'of greed and treachery and betrayal . . . yes, Kate, all human life lies behind the enigma of Sheena Franks-Walters.'

'Does it?' inquired Kate, startled and impressed.

'Yes, Kate. All human emotion is there. Come on.' She brushed away another tear.

By the following Wednesday, although she was still petrified, Mrs Bunce's pride that her little Annabel should be mixing with such people and bringing them to tea had grown intense. She had modestly acquainted the rest of Badger's Close with the fact, referring to the expected guests as 'Annabel's friends, the Franks-Walters'.

She had cleaned the house from top to bottom and prepared various cold snacks, as advised for that time of day by *That Special Guest*. She had also thoroughly absorbed the *How-To-Do-It* book on *Entertaining with Panache*. She had learned, for instance, that if one has especially important or interesting guests, the clever hostess does not waste their time with small talk, but directs the conversation to more stimulating matters. Though subtly of course for, equally, the wise hostess never monopolizes the conversation.

Thus, Mrs Bunce was as prepared as she was ever likely to be. Mr Bunce was skulking safely at work.

The Franks-Walters arrived in the limousine and every curtain in Badger's Close lifted, including Mrs Bunce's. She and Annabel and Kate – for Annabel had insisted that Kate be present, too – watched through the window as Mrs Franks-Walters stepped first from the car while Bennion held the door open for her. She was wearing her mink coat and a huge and extraordinary hat, also made of mink.

The car was so long that the rear of it protruded in front of the Pipers' drive. Kate heard their window open.

'I hope you're not stopping there,' Mrs Piper was heard to call. 'My husband'll be coming back from work soon.'

'Oh, move along, Bennion,' said Mrs Franks-Walters, irritably.

'Didn't I tell you?' said Mr Franks-Walters, following her out of the car. 'It's the warm human contact that I like. This is the sort of thing we miss at Addendon Court.'

Mrs Franks-Walters was hesitating, looking about her in some bewilderment. 'Where do we go?' she asked. 'Does it matter which entrance we use?'

'Oh, Mummy, there's only one,' said Sheena, making her 'tutting' face as she got out of the car, too. 'That one. Number nine.'

'I don't know what I'm doing here, anyway,' said Mrs Franks-Walters, a little petulantly. 'Why was I talked into coming here?'

To Mrs Bunce's horror, Annabel opened the window at that point and shouted: 'This way, Mrs Franks-Walters, straight ahead. You can't miss us.'

Mrs Franks-Walters blundered vaguely forward and then, as if caught by sudden suction, entered the drive followed by her husband and daughter.

'Fascinating, isn't it,' Mr Franks-Walters was saying, looking about him.

'I did tell you, didn't I, Daddy,' said Sheena.

Mrs Bunce opened the door. 'Welcome to our home,' she said, tremulously.

'Mum, this is Mr and Mrs Franks-Walters and

Sheena,' said Annabel. 'Mr and Mrs Franks-Walters and Sheena, this is Mum.'

'Delighted to meet you,' said Mr Franks-Walters. 'Heard a lot about you.' Everyone's hands got in a tangle as they all reached out at once.

'I'll take your hat and coat,' said Annabel to Mrs Franks-Walters. She helped her off with them, hung the coat over the banister knob, giving it a tug to make sure it stayed on, then stuck the hat on top of it, giving that a jerk too.

The hall was rather crowded and Mrs Franks-Walters, looking at a loss, wandered through into the living-room. Mr Franks-Walters went in after her, followed by Sheena who was uttering exclamations of fascination.

'You've just entered the drawing-room,' Annabel informed them. 'The dining-room's the other end and the bit in the middle is the sitting-room.'

Mrs Franks-Walters blundered through to the rear window.

'Does it stop here?' she said, peering helplessly, 'or is that yours as well over there?'

Annabel went and peered, too.

'That's the back of Brock's Gardens you're looking at,' she said. 'Those houses belong to other people.'

'Gracious!' said Mrs Franks-Walters.

'Can't remember when I've enjoyed myself quite so much,' Mr Franks-Walters was muttering. He was looking about him, taking a great interest in everything, picking things up and examining them.

'Would you like to help yourselves,' said Annabel's mother, tremulously indicating the table on which was laid the results of several days' planning and work. 'It's a buffet.'

'Wonderful!' said Mr Franks-Walters, absently, 'wonderful!' He drew Annabel aside.

'That picture,' he said, 'the one I accidently threw

away. Sheena tells me that you've stuck it on a lampshade. Now, as she explained, that picture is very dear to me but of course I quite understand about the lampshade. So I've taken the liberty of bringing one with me to put in its place. It's a very lovely lampshade. It's in the car. I only have to call to Bennion and he'll bring it in.'

He looked at her with desperate hope.

'I wonder if you've thought any more about whether you can help Mr Loader to get that grazing land for his donkey,' replied Annabel, innocently.

His face sagged and he looked profoundly depressed. Clearly, his offer had been more in hope than expectation. If, before, there had been some possibility that they had simply got their wires crossed, that it only needed a little sorting out, it had gone. They understood each other perfectly.

'I wish I could,' he said, 'but I can't.' He sighed and his face sagged even further.

'Sandwich?' inquired Mrs Bunce nervously, offering him a plate.

'Oh – oh, thanks,' he muttered. The sandwich was a rolled-up slice of thin white bread, an art almost perfected by Mrs Bunce that morning but not quite. An asparagus tip, covered in mayonnaise, slid out on to the carpet as he took it.

'I'm sorry,' he said, 'so sorry.' He bent down and picked it up, then stood not knowing what to do with it. Covered in confusion, Mrs Bunce found a plate. Then he brightened.

'Better wash my hands,' he said, 'if I may – where's the bathroom?'

'It's upstairs,' said Mrs Bunce. 'Second on the left. After Annabel's room.'

He brightened still further and hurried out of the room. There was the sound of him tripping over the first step of the stairs in his haste.

'What's going on?' Kate asked, joining Annabel.

'Sheena's father's getting excited,' replied Annabel. 'You look after Sheena, Kate.' She was listening.

Sheena was whispering: '. . . just like us in some ways, aren't they, Mummy . . .'

Mrs Franks-Walters was turning to Annabel's mother and saying: 'My compliments to your cook, Mrs Bunce,' as she sampled the tinned asparagus. 'A good cook is worth more than gems, these days, don't you agree?'

'Oh, *Mummy*!' breathed Sheena in exasperation.

Kate went over and joined them.

From upstairs, Annabel heard, faintly, a door open and close. She went out into the hall and listened again. Then she climbed the stairs quite noisily and opened the door of her room. She noticed that her lampshade decorated with coloured photographs, which she had made some months ago, was missing from the lamp in the corner. She went over and opened the wardrobe door and Mr Franks-Walters stepped out, red-faced.

'Just looking the house over,' he explained. 'Fascinating to see how other people live. Charming room. Charming wardrobe. I envy you.'

Annabel didn't even comment upon the fact that he was holding one hand to his chest where the jacket bulged out spectacularly. She could have suggested to him that there might be a connection between that and the missing lampshade but she didn't bother. The sweat was standing out on his brow and perhaps she didn't want to see him suffer any more.

'I'll show you over the rest of the house,' she offered. 'That's Mum's and Dad's room across the landing. They've got the most lovely wardrobe. If you think this one's nice you should see theirs. I'll take the clothes out if you like so that you can see it better.'

'Later, perhaps, thank you,' said Mr Franks-

Walters. He now seemed to be in a tearing hurry. He closed the wardrobe door behind him. 'Your mother will be missing me. Tea.'

He shot out of the room and there was a staccato noise on the stairs. He must have skidded down them. However, there was no final thud or cry of pain so presumably he was all right. Annabel shrugged her shoulders, closed the wardrobe door and left the room. He had disappeared altogether by the time she got out on to the landing.

He was eating a cream cheese canapé when Annabel entered the living-room. The bulge under his jacket had gone. Annabel found that of mild interest. How could it have vanished just like that? She noticed that he was shaking.

Sheena wasn't there. Annabel caught a glimpse of her through the window. She was out in the back garden with Kate, presumably making a last desperate search for something throbbing and vital.

Annabel's mother and Mrs Franks-Walters were deep in conversation.

'I suppose Fabian's adequate enough for a place like Addendon,' Mrs Franks-Walters was saying, 'but that Natalie creature is quite ridiculous. She nearly burnt my head off the other day. And when I'm trying to get her to pass me *Country Life* she hands me some comic or other. I'm always resolving to give up having my hair done in Addendon altogether and stick to the West End. Don't you feel the same, Mrs Bunce? Look, it's ridiculous my calling you Mrs Bunce. What's your Christian name?'

'Betty,' said Annabel's mother, shyly. 'Short for Elizabeth.'

'Well, Betty, if you'd like the name of my Mayfair hairdresser, who I really can recommend, just let me know.'

'Thank you, Mrs Franks-Walters –'

'Dolly, short for Dorothy. Frightfully old-fashioned name, now, isn't it!'

'Thank you, Mrs – Mrs – Dolly. It's funny, I get a bit fed up at the *Smart Set* as well. One time I went, one of Natalie's false eyelashes fell off while she was washing my hair and it stuck in my nose. She didn't even notice. It really tickled . . .'

Mrs Bunce became aware that Mr Franks-Walters was standing silently by them and that she had fallen into the very trap of which she had been warned by *Entertaining with Panache*.

'Oh, Mr Franks-Walters, you must excuse me for this trivial small talk. I've been hoping to learn about your policy when you were a junior Minister. What was it you were Minister of? You left it quite suddenly, didn't you, if I remember rightly. Was it on principle?'

'I think we ought to go,' said Mr Franks-Walters, very soon after.

'Oh, Daddy, but we've only just arrived,' said Sheena, coming in through the door again.

'I've just remembered your mother's got her Women's Institute committee meeting.'

'My what?' said Mrs Franks-Walters.

'Your Women's Institute committee meeting,' hissed Mr Franks-Walters, steering her into the hall. He looked even more nervous than before.

'That's a pity,' said Mrs Bunce, nonplussed. 'They've hardly eaten anything.'

Mr and Mrs Franks-Walters could be heard quarrelling in the hall.

'Put it *on*,' Mr Franks-Walters was muttering. 'Put it on and shut up.' Then, in a different tone of voice, 'Goodbye, Mrs Bunce. Thank you so much. You must come to Addendon Court. Goodbye, Annabel and – er –'

'What's he in such a hurry for?' said Sheena, petulantly. 'I don't know what's going on.'

She padded out, followed by Annabel, Kate and Mrs Bunce. Mr and Mrs Franks-Walters were already almost at the car. Kate thought there was something funny about Mrs Franks-Walters' head. Sheena noticed it, too. So did most of Badger's Close for every curtain was now drawn back again.

'Mummy, Mummy wait,' called Sheena. 'What are you wearing? You've got something on under your hat.' She trotted towards the car.

'I *told* you! Didn't I?' said Mrs Franks-Walters to her husband and put her hand up to her head.

'Oh, come *on*,' he said and attempted to seize her elbow and pull her into the car.

'Get off,' she said. She pushed him away.

'Oh, Mummy, it's a *lampshade*,' said Sheena. Her face looked as if it were about to explode. '*Mummy!*'

'Yes, that's my lampshade,' said Annabel, joining the group. So that was where it had disappeared to. He must have stuck it on the banister knob, wedged under his wife's hat.

'You see, it's the girl's lampshade,' said Mrs Franks-Walters, irritably. She took it off and handed it to Annabel. 'There you are, I don't know what my husband thinks he's up to. I sometimes wish he'd grow up, I really do.'

As Annabel's hand closed on one side, Mr Franks-Walters' closed on the other. On principle, Annabel tugged. Mr Franks-Walters tugged harder. He pulled it from her hand.

'Get in,' he said to his wife and flung her into the rear seat, jumping in behind her and almost landing on her. 'You ugly great brute,' she cried and started hitting him with her bag. He pulled the door to.

'Step on it, Bennion,' he was heard to order and the car shot forward under the fascinated gaze of Badger's

Close while his wife continued to hit him with her bag. Mrs Bunce had paled, realizing that there were gaps in *Entertaining with Panache*. It had failed to foresee every situation.

'*Daddy*,' yelled Sheena, stamping her foot. 'Daddy. You've gone off without me.'

The car came reversing all the way back down Badger's Close a few moments later, as Annabel had thought it might. Mr Franks-Walters lowered the window and peered out, haggardly. His wife was sitting staring furiously ahead.

'The picture isn't on the lampshade,' he complained to Annabel.

'I know,' replied Annabel. 'I took it off.' (It had never been on, in fact, but she felt that a certain amount of artistic licence was reasonable.)

'Well, you didn't ask me, did you?' she said, after a time, as he just sat looking at her, hopelessly.

He handed the lampshade to her through the window silently.

'It's not much good now, is it,' she said, in an injured tone. 'It's all squashed. It looks as if somebody's been carrying it under their jacket.'

'You'd better have this one as well, then,' he said. 'Would you hand me that lampshade on the front seat, Bennion?'

'That's *lovely*,' said Annabel, glowing with pleasure as a further lampshade was passed out to her. 'Look, Kate. Look, Mum. This is my lucky day, isn't it.'

'I'll have a word with the Managing Director of the Hackney and Wester Ross soon,' said Mr Franks-Walters. 'This evening, I expect, if I can catch him in.'

Mr Franks-Walters looked terrible.

'May I get in now?' demanded Sheena, coldly.

Chapter 8

*****

On the following Monday, Annabel and Kate were walking down the High Street together after leaving school when a large and familiar figure came backing out of a shop doorway in front of them. It was Mrs Stringer, carrying a box of groceries. They paused to help her.

'Thank you,' she puffed. 'Most kind. My car's over there. This is most fortuitous. I was just about to come round and see you. Mr Franks-Walters asked me to pass a message on to you. He was quite pressing about it.' Mrs Stringer frowned. She was clearly baffled.

'About what?' said Annabel.

'The plot of land on Stumbury. Mr Franks-Walters seems to know that you're interested, though I can't think how. Anyway, there was a planning application, just as we thought, but it's been formally withdrawn. It's quite amazing. Apparently the land is being given to Mr Loader instead. I just don't understand it. The land itself is worth a small fortune and as for what it would be worth with a shopping centre … I imagine Mr Loader will graze that scruffy, violent donkey of his on it.'

'I expect he will,' said Annabel. 'Mind you,' she added, 'his hens will probably run on it as well.'

'And he can grow his vegetables there, can't he,' said Kate.

'Quite,' said Annabel. '*And* rationalize his business in secondhand building materials. I think Addendon's got plenty of shops already. Mr Loader can make much better use of it.'

'In here,' said Mrs Stringer, opening her boot. 'Thank you. Oh, of course I'm absolutely delighted that this shopping centre has been put a stop to – and about Mr Loader, too – but I'm quite bewildered by it. It seems to me that it's a quite extraordinary triumph for Mr Franks-Walters. Quite extraordinary.'

'Do you think so?' asked Annabel.

'Oh, indeed,' said Mrs Stringer. She looked at Annabel with some smugness. 'As I remember, you made some slighting remark about Mr Franks-Walters when I saw you last and I had to put you right. You can now see for yourself what sort of man he is. A fine man, a man of the people. He has pulled this off quite alone. He must have worked amazingly hard.'

She slammed the boot lid.

'His daughter goes to your school, doesn't she?' she said.

'She's in our class,' said Annabel.

Mrs Stringer nodded approvingly. 'Well, thank you so much,' she said. 'Most kind of you. But I hope this will be a lesson to you.' She put her finger alongside her nose and nodded knowingly. 'Your elders sometimes do know better than you young people. We're not always such old fools as we look, you know.'

Mr Loader was taking down the lapboard fence when Annabel and Kate arrived to congratulate him. Eastbourne was standing patiently at his shoulder, waiting to move back into his old haunts. The hens were hanging about, too. It looked like a queue waiting for the cinema to open.

'So you've heard,' he said. He looked dazed. 'Can't quite believe it yet. Haven't got any papers or anything like that yet but I got a message from Mr Franks-Walters through Mrs Stringer. He says the land's mine bar the formalities and it's all right to go ahead and take the fence down. Do you think it's all right?'

'If Mr Big says it's all right then it is,' said Annabel. 'I mean, Mr Franks-Walters.'

'Yes, the word of a gentleman like him is good enough for anybody. I haven't heard anything direct but I think he must have been working very hard on this property company – what's its name? – the Hackney and Wester Ross. He knows all about it. Breeding will out, you see. He looks after the people, does Mr Franks-Walters.' Mr Loader shook his head admiringly. 'His daughter goes to your school, doesn't she. She's in your class.'

'Yes,' said Annabel.

He looked at Annabel and Kate shyly.

'It was you that put him up to it, wasn't it. I've cottoned on to that. I thought you had a look in your eye when you left me that day. You did it through his daughter, did you?'

'Sort of,' said Annabel.

'Thanks,' he said. 'If there's ever anything –' He looked embarrassed. 'I'll just take this bit of fence down,' he said.

Helped by Annabel and Kate, he heaved at the fence, lifting it, then lowered it to the ground. They stood aside.

Eastbourne moved through, a monarch repossessing his kingdom. Annabel gave him a pat as he went past. The cockerel strutted in after him. In his wake went the hens. Behind came the cat, stretching and holding its tail aloft. Just when it seemed the procession had finished, another hen emerged from the depths of the old blacksmith's shop accompanied by a file of chicks. They went in, too.

'I'm thinking of getting a few sheep,' said Mr Loader. He was already planning for the future.

The Goosemarket had gone, but in the shape of Mr Loader and his menagerie, the spirit of old Addendon would linger on for a while.

'Well, that settles that very satisfactorily,' Kate commented as they left.

'As soon as everything's signed, I'll send Mr Franks-Walters his picture back,' said Annabel. 'But not before,' she added, thoughtfully.

'Have we resolved the enigma of Sheena Franks-Walters though?' asked Kate.

'I think we have,' said Annabel. But although Kate looked at her inquiringly, she didn't elaborate.

It so happened that 3G had Mrs da Susa for RE the following morning and she told them the story from Genesis, Chapter 22, of how Abraham was tempted by God and told to take his only son, Isaac, to a mountain and there to sacrifice him as a burnt offering.

In sonorous tones, Mrs da Susa read:

And Abraham took the wood of the burnt offering and laid it upon Isaac, his son; and he took the fire in his hand and a knife; and they went both of them together.
And Isaac spake unto Abraham his father and said, My father: and he said, Here am I, my son.
And he said, Behold the fire and the wood: but where is the lamb for the burnt offering?

Mrs da Susa looked up and surveyed the class.

'Imagine it,' she said. 'Try to put yourself in the place of Abraham that day. Imagine his feelings as he climbed that mountain in the land of Moriah, knowing that it was his only son he was about to sacrifice, his own, innocent son, looking at him with big, trusting eyes.'

Sheena was seated placidly at the desk which she had to herself, regarding Mrs da Susa with the benign, sweet expression that she habitually wore. Annabel glanced across at her.

'Just like Sheena,' she murmured to Kate and sighed.

'Yes,' repeated Mrs da Susa. 'His own son, struggling under the weight of the wood, those faggots of firewood, not realizing that they were for him.'

'*Just* like Sheena,' nodded Annabel. 'That's what she's doing at Willers, Kate. She's her father's burnt offering. That's the solution to the enigma of Sheena Franks-Walters. We've resolved it.'

'But Mr Franks-Walters hasn't been tempted, has he?' whispered Kate, puzzled.

'Mr Franks-Walters is tempted every day, though not by the Lord!' Annabel sighed. 'Sending Sheena to slum it with the rest of us is what makes him able to meet his own eye in the mirror every morning. It means everybody can say "he's a man of the people" and believe it. Even himself.'

She sighed again.

'I suppose we could get him into a lot of trouble but what's the point? I wouldn't want to deprive Sheena of her smoked salmon sandwiches, would you, Kate? And we can't bring the Goosemarket back. We'll never know it now. It's gone forever. And, anyway, if they hadn't built our estate, we'd never have met and become friends, would we, Kate?'

That was a thought. 'No,' said Kate. 'I suppose we wouldn't.'

'I believe,' said Mrs da Susa, sternly, 'that someone is talking over there. Will you please stop.'

'So let the enigma remain,' murmured Annabel, in ·

a barely audible voice. 'Sheena will go on and on, carrying her faggots up the mountain.'

'Poor old Sheena!'

Saint Annabel

*****

Chapter 1

*****

'Have a fruit gum,' said Tracey Cooke.

There were murmurs of appreciation as she started to pass the packet round.

'Can I have a black one?' giggled Julia Channing.

'No. I like the black ones myself and they're my fruit gums,' said Tracey, firmly.

'Bad luck, Julia,' said Angela Dill. 'I like the black ones as well but I'm stuck with a rotten old yellow one.'

There were six people to share the fruit gums. Besides Tracey, Julia and Angela there were Annabel Bunce, Kate Stocks and Vicky Pearce. They were all walking back into school after the lunch break.

Annabel took hers, a red one, and began to chew it silently. Kate's was green.

'Are you putting them away again?' asked Annabel, as Tracey started to return the remaining fruit gums to her pocket. She spoke rather severely, so much so that Tracey was a little startled.

Well, yes,' said Tracey.

'A really unselfish person would have offered *all* of them round,' suggested Annabel.

'Oh,' said Tracey.

'Apart from which, as the hostess, you shouldn't really be keeping the best colours for yourself. You should be putting your guests first.'

'Oh,' said Tracey again. She paused just outside the

school doorway and rather sheepishly offered the packet round again.

'Thanks, Tracey,' said Julia, in some surprise. Fingers reached out again.

'It's not that I blame you,' said Annabel. 'Don't think that. The whole world's selfish and corrupt and it's very difficult fighting against it. *And* our teachers set us a rotten example. I know I'm just as bad myself if not worse than anybody but I suppose one's got to try to make a stand.'

She reached for a fruit gum.

'Yes,' she said. 'One can only try.'

She seemed almost to be speaking to herself, hardly aware of the others. Wrapped in thought, she placed the fruit gum in her mouth and slowly entered the school.

'She's just taken the last one!' said Tracey Cooke indignantly. '*And* it was a black one.'

Annabel was behaving most oddly. Kate had been the first to notice it but it was now becoming apparent to others, too. Annabel had adopted a new attitude to life, not quietly but ostentatiously.

It had first been brought to the general attention after Damian Price had burst a balloon outside the door of a classroom in which Mrs Jesty was giving a history lesson and then run off laughing. Annabel had lectured him for several minutes, telling him how rude it had been, particularly to someone of Mrs Jesty's age, whose nerves were no doubt rather delicate.

This had been a bit rich coming from Annabel who was perpetually shouting and laughing and banging about in the corridor but Damian Price had been so astounded that he had failed to point this out.

That had been on the previous day. It was now Tuesday and Annabel was continuing to lecture impartially. 'Oh, look, Kate,' she said now as they made their way to the chemistry lab for the first lesson of the afternoon, 'they're quarrelling again.'

'They' were Mrs Jesty and Mr Ribbons, the physics teacher. They were standing to one side of the corridor arguing in controlled voices, Mrs Jesty tossing her head and snorting, while Mr Ribbons' beard waggled furiously. This was by no means an uncommon sight in the Lord Willoughby's corridors. The quarrel was no doubt over some absurdly trivial point of school procedure or discipline.

'I'm going to have a word with them,' said Annabel.

To Kate's astonishment, she went over and joined them. Mrs Jesty and Mr Ribbons must have been equally taken aback because instead of telling her to clear off they simply looked at her dazedly.

Kate could hear only fragments. '. . . wondered if I could help . . .' was one, followed by – Annabel's finger was wagging at this point '. . . not setting a good example.'

'Oh, it's quite all right, thanks,' Kate heard Mr Ribbons mutter vaguely and both teachers went sheepishly off in opposite directions, apparently stunned.

Annabel returned looking satisfied.

That afternoon she lectured, to various people at various times, upon doing homework on time, upon gluttony and upon not cheeking teachers and making unnecessary difficulties for them since, after all, even if they did appear to lead rather idle, parasitical lives it was quite possible that there might be some truth in their claims that they did a lot of work at home. Anyway, it was right to be charitable and give them the benefit of the doubt.

Annabel was not merely talking, however. She was producing her own homework, immaculate and on time. She was holding doors open for people even when – especially when – they didn't want them held open. She had become in every way a model of rectitude. It was noticeable, too, that apart from the lectures she seemed altogether more thoughtful and reflective.

So what had brought about this conversion? What light had she seen upon the road to Damascus? Questions were being asked at Lord Willoughby's.

'What's the matter with her?' said Angela Dill to Kate in the cloakroom that afternoon as they were about to go home. 'You must know.'

But Kate didn't know. When questioned on the subject, Annabel was evasive.

Kate tried again as they made their way homewards along Church Lane.

'Annabel,' she began, 'this – this new attitude of yours. I keep getting asked about it – I mean, why –?'

'Honestly, Kate,' replied Annabel, 'is it necessary to have a reason to mend one's ways? The world's a sorry place if it is.'

Kate had been thinking of reminding her of the solemn pact they had made some time ago to share all secrets but Annabel's tone of voice suggested that on this occasion it would be pointless. Annabel fell to brooding and Kate, a little hurt, didn't feel like talking either so they continued along Church Lane in silence.

'Anyway,' said Annabel, breaking it at last, 'they shouldn't be so nosey. I've been wondering whether nosiness is a sin.'

There was a discussion about Annabel next day. It took place at the end of an English lesson. Kate was present but Annabel wasn't, having gone off in pursuit of Mr Toogood to check some point about the English homework.

There was general agreement that, whatever the

82

reason for Annabel's new saintly approach to life, it wouldn't last long, that it would falter at the first real test. There was some speculation as to when this would be and Richard White said he was open to bets.

Julia Channing, Annabel's old enemy, dropped giggling hints that if she could possibly see a way of provoking such a test she would take great pleasure in doing so.

In fact the test was to come, out of the blue, the very next day. It was to be a test of a very high order. At stake would be a visit to the sweet factory of Messrs Jackson and Hodges and, as if this were not enough, it would also entail turning the other cheek. To whom? To Julia Channing, no less.

A labour worthy of Hercules!

Chapter 2

*****

The Jackson and Hodges sweet factory had been opened on the Addendon industrial estate some two months earlier and at the time the firm had announced a competition to help promote good relations in the locality. Anyone in the area of the age of fourteen or under had been invited to compose a slogan praising Jackson and Hodges' products and to send it to them, together with a number of sweet wrappers. For the person who composed the best slogan, the prize would be a tour of the factory accompanied by a friend of their choice. In addition, the slogan, artistically lettered and framed, would be hung on the wall of the managing director's office and also printed in the firm's literature.

It was understood that a tour of the sweet factory would comprise much more than merely walking around it, watching people at work, of interest though that would be. There would be free samples, both to eat there and take away, and also a celebratory tea with the Promotions Director, at which all sorts of goodies would flow freely.

There had, therefore, been a considerable amount of interest. Annabel was, in any case, a fan of the whole range of Jackson and Hodges products, from their Chocolate Chunkles to their Grandmother Jackson's Old-Fashioned Fudge and she had been able to put genuine feeling into thinking of a slogan.

It was Miles Noggins who had first brought the competition to general attention. Entering the classroom at the end of the dinner break one day, Annabel and Kate had been confronted by the extraordinary sight of him sitting hunched at his desk, frowning and concentrating, apparently hard at work.

Peering over his shoulder to find out what subject it was that had inspired this extraordinary phenomenon, Annabel had seen that he had laboriously written in his maths exercise book (which was otherwise very little soiled by half a term's use):

Choclates and fudges and bomboms and spise
Are really nice

This message, though ill-spelt, was incontrovertibly true in substance but hardly worth spending a dinner break committing to paper and Annabel had questioned him closely. He had been reluctant to disclose what he was doing, probably sensing that his only hope of winning the competition would be if no one else were to enter, leaving him an absolutely clear field.

However, he had broken down under Annabel's probings just as Julia Channing and others had entered the room and they had all come crowding round criticizing Miles's work and making suggestions of their own.

Julia had sneered at the spelling of chocolates and bonbons and spice, pointed out that it didn't scan and that, anyway, Jackson and Hodges didn't make spices. Angela Dill said that spices weren't a particular sort of sweet, just sweets, so it was all right. Richard White had said why did it have to scan. Annabel had said that none of that mattered and the only thing that did was that Miles hadn't mentioned Jackson and Hodges by name, which destroyed the point of the thing altogether, certainly as far as

Jackson and Hodges were concerned. Miles hadn't thought of that and his mouth sagged open despairingly as he considered the daunting complexities of literary composition and how ill-fitted his mind was to cope with them.

In the hubbub, Julia had shrieked:

'Jackson and Hodges, Jackson and Hodges,
'Their sweets are so nice they make everyone podges.'

The hubbub had instantly broken out again with a babble of amendments from various quarters – 'so nice they make us all podges' – and so on, while Miles Noggins, giving up all hope, had slumped gloomily back in his seat. Julian Parlane, who had brains, was pointing out that such a slogan would hardly be likely to please Messrs Jackson and Hodges when in the midst of it all, Annabel's voice was heard to cry:

'Chocolates and toffees and bonbons and fudges
Taste better when made by Jackson and Hodges.'

This was the slogan which she had duly sent off and which now, two months later, she learned had won her the coveted prize. The letter from the firm's Promotions Director, informing her of it, arrived in the post before she left for school.

It was the morning of the fourth day of her life since her new attitude towards it had begun.

Annabel's immediate reaction was to forget about her new attitude to life and take the letter to school showing it to everyone whilst babbling about how many sweets, of what variety, she and Kate would get through, for of course Kate would be the friend who would accompany her. Naturally Kate was as excited as she was.

Whilst this was going on, Julia Channing was seen

to be walking about with her head in the air, her face slightly flushed. It could have been mistaken for pique but apparently it was not for at morning break she offered her congratulations to Annabel briefly but with dignity.

It wasn't until lunch-time when, in any case, Annabel was calming down and remembering her new attitude to life, that Julia struck her blow. Or, at least, Kate thought she struck a blow. Annabel looked at it differently.

Annabel was once more re-reading her letter from Jackson and Hodges, seated on the bench with Kate beside her, when Julia approached and sat down, too. Her face wore a curious expression, a mixture of simpering ingratiation and martyrdom.

'I've been plucking up courage all morning to ask you something,' she said to Annabel, coyly. 'It's something I wouldn't dream of doing if it were for myself. Even though it's only fair.'

'What's only fair?' asked Annabel, graciously, folding up the Jackson and Hodges letter and trying to look impartial.

'It's about the competition,' said Julia. 'I wouldn't ask if it were for myself but it – it's not . . .'

'Ask what?' said Annabel, encouragingly, as Julia faltered. 'Don't be afraid to say what's in your mind, Julia.'

'It's the competition,' said Julia. 'I suppose you think I didn't rush to congratulate you. I suppose it might have looked a bit – a bit–'

'Not at all,' said Annabel. 'It didn't look like that at all.'

It was clear to Kate that Julia was putting on a corny act and she waited patiently to see what it was all about. Presumably Annabel was leading her on, the better to demolish her.

'No,' said Julia, 'I have to confess it, Annabel,

87

there's no use my trying to hide it, I was rather put out – no, don't say anything – no, I really was. You see, I suppose I've been smarting under a sense of injustice ever since you sent in your entry for the competition and – and when your entry won, I suppose the hurt really became a little bit too much to bear –'

'Injustice?' inquired Annabel.

'Well, that slogan you sent in. It was really me who thought of it, wasn't it. I've tried to tell myself that you didn't hear me say it just a moment before you repeated it. I've really tried to make myself believe that because I know that no one would have been mean enough to steal my slogan. Especially not you, Annabel.'

Julia was becoming agitated, wriggling and bouncing up and down. Kate rolled her eyes heavenwards and waited for Annabel to deal the death-blow.

However, Annabel appeared in no hurry. She was allowing her to ramble on, presumably calculating that the satisfaction would be greater, the further Julia stuck her head into the noose.

'Go on,' she said encouragingly, as Julia showed signs of stumbling.

'That being so,' said Julia, 'and I wouldn't ask this for myself, I really wouldn't Annabel, it's because – because – but, anyway, I wondered if you could let me go to Jackson and Hodges in your place. I feel – perhaps you feel – that you owe it to me.'

Incredibly, Annabel did not push her to the ground there and then. Instead, even more incredibly, her expression softened.

'If you're not asking for yourself, who are you asking for?' she said.

'My little cousin,' said Julia, her voice breaking cornily just as she'd seen ham actresses do it on television. 'She's in hospital.'

'Your little cousin?' inquired Annabel. 'But I don't quite understand, Julia. You mean, you want her to go to the sweet factory –?'

'Oh, no,' said Julia hastily, 'she couldn't do that. In any case, she can't move.'

'Why?' asked Annabel, sympathetically. 'What's the matter with her?'

'Both legs broken, strapped to the ceiling, doctors not sure she'll ever walk again,' replied Julia rapidly. She seemed anxious to get away from the subject. 'But you see, I'd be able to take her some sweets and tell her all about the visit and how the sweets are made. It would bring a tiny bit of joy into her life.'

This was clearly the moment for Annabel to deliver the blow. Surely it could be held off no longer. Instead, Annabel said gravely:

'Very well, Julia, you shall go to the sweet factory in my place. I shall write a letter to Jackson and Hodges explaining that the slogan was really your idea. You and Kate will go together.'

'What?' cried Kate.

'What?' cried Julia. 'Oh, Annabel, I shall be eternally grateful –'

'Not at all,' said Annabel. 'It is your due. Now I should go if I were you and tell your little cousin.'

'Oh, I shall!' cried Julia. 'I know she'll mention you in her prayers tonight, Annabel. You won't forget, will you – about the letter.'

'Of course not. It's history first lesson, isn't it? Mrs Jesty. I shall write it then.'

'Oh, thank you, thank you, Annabel!'

'Annabel! You can't do this!' said Kate, as Julia made off.

'Eh? Why not, Kate,' said Annabel, looking at her abstractedly as if her mind were elsewhere.

'Why *not*? You're not paying any attention to that nonsense, are you, Annabel. She's making it all up.

She'll go to the sweet factory then giggle about it all round the school.'

Annabel frowned. 'Really, Kate,' she said, disapprovingly. 'It does you no credit to speak ill of –'

'Annabel, even if you want her to go to the sweet factory for some reason, think of me. I don't want to go with *her*. It'd spoil everything –'

Annabel looked alarmed.

'Kate. I didn't think you'd be selfish. It's not much to ask, is it. Think of her little cousin –'

'Oh, *Annabel*!' said Kate. She glanced round to see that Julia, who was walking away in the direction of the school building, was moving with a rather stilted gait, fighting hard to keep a joyful spring out of her step. Once around the corner out of sight she would no doubt give vent her to feelings with several leaps for joy.

'This'll make her even worse,' said Kate, despairingly. 'If that's possible. It certainly won't do her any good.'

'Won't do her any good?' repeated Annabel, with a frown. 'What do you mean, Kate?'

'Well, obviously –' began Kate. But Annabel interrupted.

'Her teeth,' said Annabel. 'That's what you're thinking about, isn't it. You're right, Kate, you're always so right about everything. No, I certainly wouldn't want Julia to ruin her teeth with all those sweets.'

She half rose from her seat.

'Julia!' she called.

Julia had almost reached the corner. At the sound of Annabel's voice she paused, the spring dying out of her step. Then slowly she turned. Evidently she thought her luck had run out, that Annabel, having toyed with her, was now about to deliver the *coup de grâce*.

'You will think about your teeth, won't you, Julia,' called Annabel. 'And your little cousin's. Try not to eat too many of the really sticky ones, won't you. Some of those toffees and fudges can be really destructive.'

'I'll certainly bear that in mind, Annabel,' said Julia, a slow flush of joy suffusing her face again. 'Perhaps I should tend to concentrate more on the chocolates?'

'I think that would be sensible,' nodded Annabel. 'And your little cousin, of course.'

'And my little cousin, of course,' nodded Julia.

She turned and, walking even more stiltedly than before, disappeared round the corner of the building.

Kate would have liked to be transported there instantly by a magic carpet. She could visualize the scene.

Julia, triumphant, all restraint cast aside, would be dancing, flinging herself ecstatically about like some elephantine ballet dancer, a graceless, giggling, cavorting assemblage of arms and legs.

She would not be thinking about her teeth.

'You don't understand, Kate,' said Annabel, that evening. 'I want to make my peace with Julia.'

It was evening and Kate was in Annabel's room at home, trying to get to the bottom of it. Annabel, unusually for her, instead of fidgeting about, was reclining on her bed, head resting on the pillow, hand trailing over the edge of the bed. Occasionally she put her other hand to her forehead.

'I've been hoping an opportunity like this would turn up,' she said.

'I don't think, Kate, that my winning the competition can be entirely chance. I think it must be Fate. You know how I'm a great believer in Fate, don't you, and anyway there's no other explanation. That it

91

should come now – just when it was Julia that I was feeling so especially guilty about.'

'I shouldn't think she's *got* a little cousin,' said Kate, morosely.

She had watched with astonishment that afternoon as Annabel had written her letter to Jackson and Hodges, showing it to a delighted Julia before putting it in an envelope borrowed from Angela Dill – who kept a supply in her desk – upon which she stuck a stamp provided by an eagerly-helpful Julia herself. This in itself was remarkable since Julia's meanness was legendary.

Holding up the envelope she had then delivered a speech to Julia, saying that she hoped this would serve to wipe out any memories of past misunderstandings between them. It gave her the chance to atone for any little meannesses on her part which might have soiled their relationship.

Julia had enthusiastically indicated that it did and Annabel had then nipped out to the pillar box between lessons in order to post it as quickly as possible just in case, as she had explained to Kate, she was tempted by evil thoughts. She had returned empty-handed, looking tranquil.

So, apart from anything else, Kate would be stuck with Julia for company on the visit to the sweet factory. It made her want to bang her head against a wall repeatedly.

'Perhaps, Kate,' said Annabel, 'and I say this in no spirit of criticism, merely helpfulness, perhaps you should look into your relationships and wonder whether there's anything you can do too. I wish I could find the words to tell you what joy it is to make it up with Julia, to repay her in a small way for all the nasty little thoughts about her that I've allowed to enter into my mind . . .'

'Annabel,' said Kate. 'What *is* the matter?'

'And the nasty little deeds, too!' said Annabel, abstractedly.

Kate groaned.

'I wonder where I can find out if Julia's got a little cousin,' she said.

It soon became apparent to Kate that Julia, unable to contain herself, was already going around boasting that she'd got the better of Annabel and that, to the more unscrupulous element at Lord Willoughby's, Annabel was being seen as a soft touch.

'You've soiled our relationship for too long,' leered Damian Price when Annabel absent-mindedly didn't get out of his way when he tried to push into the queue for the coffee-vending machine. 'Isn't there never going to be no end to it?'

Annabel, still abstracted, let him in front of her.

That evening, Kate went triumphantly round to Annabel's house to be told by Mrs Bunce that Annabel was up in her room.

'I've hardly seen her for days,' said Mrs Bunce. 'She's spending all her time up there.'

Kate found Annabel reclining on her bed.

'Annabel,' she said with satisfaction. 'Julia hasn't got a little cousin. I told you, didn't I.'

'How do you know that, Kate?' Annabel asked gently without looking at her. 'Who told you?'

'Her mother,' said Kate, with relish. 'I called at Julia's house half-an-hour ago because I knew she'd be out – she goes to yoga classes on Fridays – and I said to Mrs Channing that I'd called just to find out how her little niece was and to see if she was any better.'

'And what did Mrs Channing say?' asked Annabel.

'She looked at me as if I were mad and said there must be a mistake. She hasn't got a little niece. She's got a nephew in London but he's eighteen and plays in the scrum in his local rugger team. She told me a lot about him. Mostly it was very boring but not all of it. Apparently the two branches of the Channing family don't get on together. The London Channings are very stand-offish and treat the Addendon Channings like dirt. They're very mean, too. They've got a boat moored at Mersea Island but they never invite the Addendon Channings to go out in it. Not that Mr and Mrs Channing care about it for themselves, just for Julia. Sailing would broaden her experience. The London Channings have always been the same. They didn't even bother to come to Julia's christening, they said it was too far. Mrs Channing thinks the London Channings might behave like this because they think the Addendon Channings aren't up to their level socially but you've only got to look at the Addendon Channings' house to see that's not true. It's the only detached house in the road *and* it hasn't just got a through lounge like the others, it's got a separate dining-room *and* a utility room which Mr Channing's done out and put a window in so that Julia can do her homework there and have her stereo equipment and use it as a den where friends can come and see her except that they don't which is such a pity. It's an *executive* house. *And* they went to Cyprus for their holidays last year which is more than the London Channings did. Mr and Mrs Channing wouldn't really have bothered for themselves, the food at the hotel was awful and the climate so hot but they feel that it's so important for Julia to see something of the world if she's to grow up a properly rounded young lady. But anyway, in spite of all this, the London Channings keep on treating them like dirt and it's very frustrating.

'The London Channings', added Kate after a pause for breath and reflection following her highly condensed précis of the earful she had received while shifting from one foot to the other on the Channings' doorstep, 'sound like very sensible people.'

'Poor Julia,' murmured Annabel, gently.

'Poor Julia!' Kate repeated in astonishment. She sat down in the chair and looked at Annabel. Annabel's eyes appeared to have misted over.

'Treated like dirt by her relatives,' murmured Annabel. 'Sitting there in her den with her stereo equipment waiting for her friends to – to – come and see her and – and nobody comes and – all this time I've been making things worse for her . . .'

'Annabel,' said Kate, 'Julia is lying to you. Not only that, she's going round laughing and telling everybody that she's made a chump out of you. She's encouraging other people to make a chump out of you as well.'

Annabel's eyes filled with tears.

'If Julia has found it necessary to tell a lie, then it shows how badly she must want to go on this tour of the sweet factory. Surely you must see that, Kate.'

'But she's just a great big cheat as usual –'

'I have cheated her so often that it's right she should cheat me now. I welcome it, Kate.'

Annabel raised herself on one elbow.

'Don't you understand, Kate? I owe it to her. Oh, Julia, poor Julia, how can I help her to make as big a chump out of me as possible? It's all I can do to repay her for everything, to wipe the slate clean . . .'

'It's not only for Julia I'm doing this, Kate. It's for others, too. The teachers and everybody. You can't expect them to behave well if they're not set an example. In my small way perhaps I can set them that example. It seems the least I can do. To make some use of my otherwise pointless and parasitical life.'

Kate went home. It was Friday evening. And she was seriously worried about Annabel.

Chapter 3

*****

Next morning she received a telephone call from Mrs Bunce. This startled her because Annabel's mother had never before telephoned her and the possibility of such an event occurring had never even entered Kate's mind. Her own mother looked surprised as she handed the phone over.

'Annabel's asking to see you,' said Mrs Bunce, in that slightly puzzled tone of voice which was almost her normal way of speaking.

'Where is she?' asked Kate in some anxiety.

'In her room. She's lying on her bed.'

'Is she all right?'

'Oh, yes. She says she's fine. Just feeling a bit tired, that's all. I can't think why. She hasn't been doing anything.'

'I'll come round straight away.'

Annabel was reclining on her bed, exactly as she had been doing on the previous evening, one hand trailing over the edge of the bed.

'Hi!' said Kate.

Annabel looked a little wan. Without at first replying, she moved over a little and then, lifting her trailing hand, patted the bed with it.

'Hallo, Kate,' she said, then added softly, 'Kate, my own Kate, sit down beside me.'

There was an alarm clock on the table by her bed which Kate didn't remember having seen there

96

previously. It had a very loud, portentous tick. Beside it lay an excercise book and biro.

'What's the matter?' said Kate, doing as she was asked.

Annabel did not at first reply. Instead, she laid the back of her hand across her eyes.

'Kate, my own Kate,' she repeated after a time, then lapsed into silence again.

Waiting patiently for some further communication, Kate idly turned over the cover of the exercise book. It was instantly snatched away by Annabel.

'Annabel, what's the matter?' asked Kate, in some exasperation.

'You're sure the door's closed?' asked Annabel. 'I know Mum and Dad are going out shopping soon but I think they're still here.'

Kate checked. It was.

'I wouldn't want to worry them,' said Annabel. 'Not that there's anything to worry about but you know what they're like. No. You're the one person I can trust, Kate. You, my friend, my great friend.'

'Trust?' said Kate, sitting down again. 'About what?'

'This is just a precaution, Kate, you needn't think it's anything more than that. But I want to ask you if you'll be my executor.'

'Your *executor*! What do you mean, your executor, what's that?'

'I don't know exactly,' said Annabel, 'but I think it means that you handle my affairs . . . if anything were to happen to me . . . if I were to get run over for instance. I want to tell you – er – who I'd want to have my things if that were to happen and then – then if it did you'd see that they – they got them.'

'What are you talking about, Annabel?' said Kate, baffled.

'I did think of seeing a solicitor,' continued

Annabel, 'but –' there was a slight catch in her voice as she said this and she waved a hand vaguely around the room – 'I thought perhaps my possessions wouldn't really be enough for that. I don't suppose a solicitor would be interested.'

Kate looked around at the collections of snail shells, birds' feathers and so on which formed the bulk of Annabel's possessions.

There was a knock at the door.

'We're off, Annabel,' came Mrs Bunce's voice. 'We won't be back till the afternoon. You're sure you'll be all right on your own?'

'I shall be perfectly all right, Mum,' Annabel assured her, raising her voice. 'In any case, Kate is with me.'

'Well, all right, dear,' replied Mrs Bunce after a moment's hesitation. 'We'll see you later. Bye, Kate.'

'Bye, Mrs Bunce.'

Mrs Bunce's footsteps were heard receding down the stairs. Within the room there was silence except for the loudly-ticking clock. It was starting to get on Kate's nerves. She heard the front door slam, then the sound of the car's engine as Mr and Mrs Bunce drove away.

'But what's this about executors, Annabel –?' Kate began.

'Now, there's no need to fuss,' said Annabel. 'Being my executor's very simple. You just take this exercise book and, as you see' – she flicked open the cover – 'on the first page there's a list of my belongings with a name against each of them. That's the name of the person they're to go to when – I mean, if anything were to happen to me.'

'Stamp album – Tracey Cooke,' Kate read out aloud.

'Tracey's keen on stamps.'

'Snail shells, sea shells and birds' feathers – Angela Dill.'

'Angela's very interested in nature.'

Kate ran her eye down the long list. Some things were surprising. One, in particular, caused her to raise her eyebrows in some astonishment.

'My rose-bush – Andrew Torrance!' she read, then realized that Annabel was blushing.

'You know the one I mean,' said Annabel, 'the one in the corner of the garden. It's called "Schoolgirl".'

Yes, Kate knew the one she meant. It had been one of her whims, planted and tended with her own hands.

'But,' said Kate, 'just supposing this – this share-out ever took place, do you mean I'd have to dig it up and take it to Andrew Torrance?'

'That sort of thing is all part of an executor's duties,' said Annabel, simply. She had her face turned away from Kate, obviously too embarrassed to meet her eye. Andrew Torrance was in the Fifth Year and Kate was well aware of the role he occupied in Annabel's thoughts.

'Supposing that after I've dug it up and taken it to him he doesn't want it –' began Kate. Then she stopped. This was looking unnecessarily far ahead. Besides, her eye had fallen upon an entry which moved her deeply. It was right at the foot of the page and read:

All else, including Beady, to my best friend, Kate.

Beady was Annabel's most treasured possession, although she didn't often care to admit it. He was her battered-eared, one-eyed teddy bear whom she had owned since she was three.

'I know you'd look after him,' said Annabel, looking away shyly again.

Kate nodded, rather overcome for the moment.

The mood was broken as her eye lighted upon

another entry, an entry so sensational that she had to read it again to make sure there was no mistake.

The Queen's Heel-tip – Julia Channing

The Queen's heel-tip was Annabel's second most prized possession and there was a long history of bitterness and quarrels over it between her and Julia Channing. This had begun some months earlier when Mrs da Susa, the Deputy Head of Lord Willoughby's, had taken a party from the Third Year to a town some thirty miles distant to see the Queen, who had been going on a walk-about there.

Annabel, Union Jack in one hand and dragging Kate along behind her with the other, had squirmed her way skilfully through the crowd, hoping to be spoken to by the Queen. At the crucial moment, however, she had been distracted by Julia Channing who had cunningly made use of Annabel's superior squirming ability by tagging along in her wake, clutching at the back of Kate's blazer and then, using surprise tactics, ruthlessly and brazenly elbowed both Kate and Annabel aside. Annabel had fought back, using her Union Jack to good effect, but unfortunately by the time she had dealt with Julia's intervention the Queen had turned and was moving away again. However, Annabel had noticed that as the Queen lifted her foot from the ground she left behind her a metal heel-tip which had apparently come off her shoe.

Julia had noticed it at the same moment and she and Annabel had both reached for it. They had fought ruthlessly for it until finally Annabel had won by pushing Julia into the arms of a policeman who was coming to see what the disturbance was about and who was unimpressed by Julia's charges that Annabel was a thief who was robbing her of valuable property, especially as Annabel was looking extremely innocent and law-abiding while these remarks were being made. Julia had received a warning to behave herself which had added to her bitterness.

Kate was, meanwhile, expressing some doubt as to whether the heel-tip had really come from the Queen's shoe anyway because surely the Queen wouldn't bother with such things. Surely she would simply have a new pair of shoes brought to her when the heels of one pair started to wear down?

A little worried by this, Annabel had gone squirming off through the crowds again in pursuit of the Queen, hoping to catch a glimpse of her other heel to see if there were a tip on that. But she had been thwarted. Just as she had been about to catch up, the Queen had got back into her car and been driven away.

However, Annabel had soon dismissed Kate's doubts and declared herself fully satisfied with the authenticity of the heel-tip. She could, in any case, hardly have done otherwise without presenting Julia with a moral victory.

(Kate herself still wasn't convinced. What she had refrained from pointing out to Annabel, because it might have been too dampening after all that had been gone through to get it, was that the heel-tip might well have come from the shoe of Mrs da Susa, whom Kate had noticed standing on the spot where it had been found before moving back under crowd pressure at the approach of the Queen.)

At home, Annabel had given the heel-tip pride of place on her dressing-table, keeping it displayed in a very attractive open box, lined with some velvety stuff of a rich, royal purple colour. The box had once housed her father's cuff-links. (He had given it to her after complaining that the spring on the lid was too strong and he always trapped his fingers painfully when trying to shut it.) In front of the box was a little card on which was typed METAL HEEL-TIP

FROM THE QUEEN'S SHOE. Kate could see it from where she sat.

'You really mean that?' said Kate, astounded. 'You'd really like to see Julia have that.'

'No one thing could do more to heal the rift between Julia and me,' said Annabel.

Kate stood up. This was going too far.

'Annabel, what's going on?' she demanded. 'What is all this?'

She was startled to see a big tear roll slowly out of Annabel's left eye.

'Annabel!' she cried.

'Can you promise not to tell anybody, Kate?' said Annabel. 'Especially not Mum and Dad.'

'Well, yes.'

'Promise. Really promise.'

'Yes. Yes anything.' Kate was quite alarmed.

'I may have to go away somewhere quite soon, Kate. I didn't want to worry anybody, especially you, Kate, and my parents. That's why I was keeping it a secret. But it's got to come out.'

'Go away somewhere? Where? What are you talking about?'

'I've got an incurable disease, Kate.'

Kate's mind grappled with the enormity of this, trying to take it in. But it was difficult.

Annabel pointed to the back of her neck.

'Feel that spot, Kate,' she said. 'Press it down, then take your finger away.'

Kate did as she was asked.

'Is the spot staying down or is it rising up again when you take your finger away?' asked Annabel in a tremulous voice.

'I – I'm not sure,' replied Kate. She found that her voice was shaking, too. 'Which is it supposed to do?'

Annabel slipped off her shoe and sock.

'Bend my big toe back,' she commanded, holding up the foot so as to facilitate the operation.

'It won't go,' said Kate. 'Not very far, anyway. Not without forcing it.'

'You see,' said Annabel.

'See what?' asked Kate.

'And there's the – the dry throat and feeling of indigestion . . .'

'But what's it all *mean*, Annabel?'

Annabel reached over and put her hand under the bed. From there she produced a very large, extremely tattered book. The dark red covers were tenuously held on with sticky tape.

'It's all in here. It's the *Bumper Home Compendium of Medicine*. I found it in the bookcase.'

Kate took it from her and turned a few pages. It had been published in 1897.

'But what have you *got*, Annabel?'

'It's on page 603,' said Annabel. 'I'll show you.' Taking the book back she started to search for a page. Then she closed it again.

'No, I can't. It's too terrible,' she said. She put the book under the pillow and laid her head on it.

'I think I want to be left alone now, Kate.'

'But –'

'I don't want you to worry at all, Kate. As far as I'm concerned I expect it will all be very beautiful. I may have to go into some sort of nursing home where I shall quietly waste away but it'll probably take quite a few years. I hope I shan't be a nuisance to anybody. I wouldn't want to be a nuisance. But, anyway, Kate, you'll see to everything for me, won't you.'

It was all clear now. Annabel's new attitude to life. Everything.

'But, Annabel –'

'Please go now, Kate. And Kate –'

'Yes, Annabel?'

'Try to think well of me.'

There was only the sound of the clock ticking. Bemused, Kate got up.

As she quietly closed the door of the room behind her, it seemed to her that the ticking came to an end. Annabel must have stopped the clock. Perhaps it had been getting on her nerves, too.

Chapter 4

*****

The vow of secrecy was all very well but the responsibility was too much. After pacing up and down the street in great agitation for five minutes, Kate decided she had to consult somebody. She went home and rang up Angela Dill.

'She's *what*?' said Angela. 'You've got to get a doctor, Kate.'

'But I made a vow of secrecy,' said Kate.

'Don't be daft,' said Angela. 'We can't let Annabel peg out because of a vow of secrecy. Still,' she said, after a pause, 'it's a bit tricky. I'll ring up Fiona and see what she thinks.' She rang off.

The telephone wires must have hummed within the next few minutes. It was Tracey Cooke who rang Kate back.

'Everybody's agreed you have to ring the doctor, Kate. You're her best friend.'

'Everybody? How many —?'

'I'm just going to her house now. I think a lot of people are. I know Julia Channing's gone already. It's terrible, isn't it, Kate.' She rang off.

There didn't seem much point in keeping the vow of secrecy any longer anyway. Kate rang up Doctor Fleming. He sounded rather suspicious at first but she managed to persuade him that it was urgent.

*

There was a crowd of people from the Third Year in the front garden of Annabel's home when Kate got there. Tracey was just arriving, too.

'Julia's gone inside,' said Vicky Pearce. 'She insisted.'

Julia emerged at that moment, looking dazed. She was holding the box with the Queen's heel-tip in it.

'She's just given me this,' she said. 'It's incredibly moving, isn't it.'

She started to close the lid which immediately snapped shut on her finger and she gave a howl of pain.

'How did she look, Julia?' asked Vicky Pearce, anxiously.

'Calm,' said Julia, sucking her finger. 'You have to hand it to her. She looked calm.'

'Wasn't she surprised to see you?' asked Kate. 'It was supposed to be a secret.'

'She was a bit,' said Julia, 'but she didn't seem to mind too much. She said at least it meant she could give me this personally.'

'Should we all go in, Kate?' asked Fiona Turnbull.

Everybody was looking at Kate, awaiting her decision. She was Annabel's friend and executor.

'I don't know,' she replied helplessly.

Tracey Cooke sniffed and the sniff developed into a sob.

'She's been a marvellous person,' she wailed, suddenly.

'In different circumstances,' said Julia, with a quiver in her voice, no doubt quoting some television saga she had seen, 'we could have been great friends.' She looked down at the box in her hand. 'I shall treasure this always not for what it is but for to whom it belonged.' She stumbled a little over the sentence but managed to get it out satisfactorily. Then she said: 'Apart from the Queen, I mean.'

Astonishingly, Damian Price and Richard White were slouching along Badger's Close to swell the crowd. How had they heard? Half of Willers would be here soon at this rate.

The window of the next door house banged open and Mrs Piper, the Bunces' right-hand neighbour, stuck her head out.

'What's going on here?' she demanded. 'What are you lot hanging about for? Go on. Shoo!'

No-one took any notice of her, however, and she was silenced by the arrival of Doctor Fleming's car.

'Stand aside,' he said irritably. 'Do I understand her parents aren't at home?'

Kate nodded numbly. 'You just walk in,' she said.

He disappeared into the house.

A hush fell upon the assembly as they waited. It was broken by Tracey Cooke.

'We should have been better to her,' she cried.

'You lot can talk,' jeered Damian Price. 'You've all been trying to make a chump out of her.'

'She was too good for us,' wailed Tracey. 'Too good for us. We didn't know. We didn't know.' She went off into another loud spasm of sobbing which sent Vicky Pearce off.

In the midst of it the door opened and Doctor Fleming emerged. He appeared to be in a great hurry, closing his bag and looking at his watch in some agitation. He walked straight past the group and was almost into his car before anyone had realized it. Kate only just managed to catch him.

'Doctor,' she called. 'Doctor – what –! What – what –!'

He paused, half into his car.

'Spots and probably eating too fast and talking too much,' he said, brusquely. 'That's what's wrong. I'm giving her a prescription for the spots. The rest is up to her. Now, if you'll excuse me, I've got a lot of other calls to make.'

He slammed the door and drove away.

There was silence. Then the door opened and Annabel appeared.

'I thought, Kate,' she said, 'that you were my friend.'

There was no anger in her voice, only hurt.

'I thought,' she said, 'that you made a vow of secrecy –'

She broke off. She was looking at something. Glancing round, Kate saw that Julia Channing, tightly clutching the box containing the Queen's heel-tip, was trying to sidle away unnoticed. She was already negotiating the gate.

'You gave it to me,' cried Julia, defensively, seeing that she had been spotted. She went off at a brisk walk.

Annabel shot in pursuit.

'You can't change your mind now,' Julia was heard to cry as Annabel caught up with her. It was the last attempt at reasoned communication before the situation deteriorated into an unsaintly scuffle with each tugging at the box containing the Queen's heel-tip.

Annabel's attitude to life, Kate realized, had returned to normal.

It was Annabel who was triumphant in the struggle. She returned, a little dishevelled, holding the box and oblivious of the abuse which Julia was sending in her wake.

Taking Kate by the arm, she led her inside the house and closed the door.

Annabel's annoyance with Kate lasted no more than a few moments because, as she said, she knew that anything Kate did would always be for the best and anyway it was impossible to contemplate there being a difference between them.

Besides, it was such a fantastic relief to know that she wasn't going to have to go off and spend years in some dreary nursing home and she'd never have had the courage to go to the doctor herself. She'd have been far too scared. And now they'd got this marvellous visit to the sweet factory to look forward to, so wasn't everything absolutely wonderful? Oh, wasn't life wonderful altogether! Only those who had walked in the shadows could know quite *how* superbly, fantastically wonderful it was.

The remark about the sweet factory puzzled Kate at first because surely Annabel had informed Jackson and Hodges that it was Julia who was to go on the tour. Surely she had posted a letter to that effect?

Annabel replied shyly that it was indeed true that she had set off to post the letter. However, on the way to the pillar box she had been overcome by a sudden yearning for some Jackson and Hodges Chocolate Chunkles. There had been no particular urgency about the letter, which could be posted at any time during the next week or so, so she had put it in her pocket and made a dash to the sweet shop instead.

Upon returning to the school, not wanting the letter to stay in her pocket any longer than was necessary because it would get creased, she had put it in her desk. Unfortunately she had forgotten about it and it was still there.

However, this had really turned out to be extremely fortunate because upon reflection it was clear that Julia was being her usual lying, cheating, cunning, unscrupulous self and the whole idea of her going to the sweet factory had been quite monstrous, especially after the sheer nerve of telling all those lies about her little cousin.

'I would like', said Annabel, again looking shyly at

Kate, 'to apologize for almost inflicting her company upon you. I wasn't myself at the time, Kate.'

Kate indicated that she understood.

The tour of Jackson and Hodges' sweet factory turned out to be all that could be desired and Annabel even brought some sweets back for Julia, which in the circumstances was quite magnanimous of her.

She also gave Julia the letter which she had forgotten to post because, she said kindly, she was sure she would want to steam the unused stamp off.

THE LANDFILL
David Leney

Danny is angry when he discovers his safe, private world among the junk at the landfill has been invaded. But he has no idea that something as innocent as a story recorded on a cassette could have such a dramatic effect on his life.

STORM BIRD
Elsie McCutcheon

Torn from her father and her London school, Jenny is sent to live with her grim and sometimes frightening aunt in a small East Anglian seaside town. She is befriended by Josh, son of her aunt's wealthy employers, and shares his secret, passionate interest in birds. But the sinister mystery of her aunt's past begins to haunt Jenny, as it does the whole village. As the web of horror and tragedy is unravelled, Jenny and Josh are thrown together in a gripping climax to this powerful and dramatic story.

MOONDIAL
Helen Cresswell

Minty has heard stories of strange happenings in the big house across the road from her Aunt's cottage. And when she walks through the gates, the lodge-keeper knows it is Minty who holds the key to the mysteries. She has only to discover the secret power of the moondial, and she will be ready to carry out the dangerous mission which awaits her . . .

A haunting and beautifully written time-travel novel, by the author of *The Secret World of Polly Flint*.

TALES FOR THE TELLING
Edna O'Brien

In *Tales for the Telling* you'll meet giants and leprechauns, heroes and princesses. Stories of love and high deeds which have been passed from generation to generation are now presented together in this colourful and charming volume. A huge tradition of Irish storytelling is now available to a new audience.

JUNIPER
Gene Kemp

Since her dad left, Juniper and her mum have had nothing but problems and now things are just getting worse – there are even threats to put Juniper into care. Then she notices two suspicious men who seem to be following her. Who are they? Why are they interested in her? As Christmas draws nearer, Juniper knows something is going to happen . . .

THE SEA IS SINGING
Rosalind Kerven

Tess lives right in the north of Scotland, in the Shetland Islands, and when she starts hearing the weird and eerie singing from the sea it is her neighbour, old Jacobina Tait, who helps her understand it. With her strange talk of whales and 'patterns' Jacobina makes Tess realize that she cannot – and must not – ignore what the singing is telling her. But how can Tess decipher the message?

RACSO AND THE RATS OF NIMH
Jane Leslie Conly

When fieldmouse Timothy Frisby rescues young Racso, the city rat, from drowning, it's the beginning of a friendship. It's also the beginning of Racso's education – and an adventure. For the two are caught up in the brave and resourceful struggle of the Rats of NIMH to save Thorn Valley, their home, from destruction.

A TASTE OF BLACKBERRIES
Doris Buchanan Smith

The moving story about a young boy who has to come to terms with the tragic death of his best friend and the guilty feeling that he could somehow have saved him.

JELLYBEAN
Tessa Duder

A sensitive modern novel about Geraldine, alias
'Jellybean', who leads a rather solitary life as the only child
of a single parent. She's tired of having to fit in with her
mother's busy schedule, but a new friend and a performance of 'The Nutcracker Suite' change everything.

THE PRIESTS OF FERRIS
Maurice Gee

Susan Ferris and her cousin Nick return to the world of O
which they had saved from the evil Halfmen, only to find
that O is now ruled by cruel and ruthless priests. Can they
save the inhabitants of O from tyranny? An action-packed
and gripping story by the author of prize-winning THE
HALFMEN OF O.

BACK HOME
Michelle Magorian

A marvellously gripping story of an irrepressible girl's
struggle to adjust to a new life. Twelve-year-old Rusty,
who had been evacuated to the United States when she
was seven, returns to the grey austerity of post-war
Britain.

THE BEAST MASTER
Andre Norton

Spine-chilling science fiction – treachery and revenge!
Hosteen Storm is a man with a mission to find and punish
Brad Quade, the man who killed his father long ago on
Terra, the planet where life no longer exists.

BOY and
GOING SOLO
Roald Dahl

The enthralling autobiography of this much-loved author, from his earliest days to his experiences as a pilot in the Second World War.

THE APPRENTICES
Leon Garfield

A collection of the much-acclaimed Apprentices stories. Each story features one London trade and is linked by recurring characters.

THE BONNY PIT LADDIE
Frederick Grice

Set in the early twentieth century, this story of a boy growing up in a mining village was one of the first children's books to show real working-class children in credible surroundings.

SARAH, PLAIN AND TALL
Patricia MacLachlan

What would she be like, this new mother found through a newspaper advertisement? And, above all, would she be able to sing?